Gusty Proposals

The Crystal Garden Saga

Gusty Proposals

Book 3 of The Crystal Garden Saga

L J Gastineau

GUSTY PROPOSALS,
BOOK 3 OF *THE CRYSTAL GARDEN SAGA*

This is a work of fiction. All characters and events portrayed are fictional, and any resemblance to real people or incidents is purely coincidental.

Cover Art by Blue
Cover Design by Doris Ross

A Trinity Gateways LLC Publication
www.TrinityGateways.net

ISBN: 0988195143
ISBN-13:   978-0988195141

Dedications

This book is dedicated to my mom who had showed me how to appreciate the beauty in the world as its own form of art. Thank you for encouraging me to pursue my craft and believing in my abilities to succeed.

Chapter 1

Where am I?
The dark forest was foreboding in the moon-less night, yet somehow she had a feeling she had been there before. It was almost like déjà vu.

Something was coming.

She could hear the snapping of twigs in the distance. Her heart raced, fearing the unknown. Should she run? Should she hide? She could barely see anything around her. Only outlines of trees; their branches skeletal and grasping as though they could snatch her from where she stood like some sort of thief of night.

Something cold and wet touched her face. Was it raining? She would have to find someplace to use as a shelter or risk getting pneumonia.

Forgetting all the mysteries that lurked in the dark she ran blindly. A glimmer caught her eye from the right. Curious, she headed in that direction then came to a halt. It was a large gilded mirror. Mesmerized by her reflection she approached it staring in wonder. A scream tore from her throat as something beyond its smooth surface grabbed her pulling her towards it.

Chapter 2

*V*iolet Piccolo gritted her teeth when the shrill cry of her alarm clock ripped her away from her dreams. She groaned, tugging her pillow over her head as she squirmed further under the covers.

Next she was greeted by a firm rapping at her bedroom door. "Violet, it's time to get up…"

She winced at the insistent sound in her mother's voice. Didn't the woman realize that it was her daughter's sixteenth birthday? Shouldn't Violet be allowed to do whatever she wished including sleeping in rather than playing dress up? She was so sick of doing everything that was expected of her!

"Violet, are you even listening to me? We have a long day ahead of us."

Knowing that unless she said something, she would have to endure a long winded lecture, the petite girl surfaced from her warm cocoon. "Okay, mother. I'll be right there."

"Wear a button down shirt, please. It'll keep your hair from getting messed up when you change for tonight."

"Okay."

Once the click of high heels departed away from the door, Violet plopped back down on the soft pillow, a halo of strawberry blonde curls fanned out around her head. She sighed, lifting her amber gaze towards her calendar. May 20th. Her birthday, yet… It felt like it had never been hers to begin with.

As the only daughter of a well-to-do businessman and his socialite wife, Violet felt she was more like a commodity. She was always expected to behave a certain way. Her friends were handpicked by her parents, from the time she could talk. Her life, in general was regulated from what she could eat to what she wore. Her birthday was no exception.

Rather than have a simple party with friends or even dinner out with her parents, Violet was expected to cater to being another pawn in her father's climb up the cooperate ladder as his boss's, son's Prom date!

What's next? Marriage? Violet glared at the garment bag which contained the baby pink gown trimmed in sparkling crystals—nothing less for her parents' little bargaining chip.

"Violet! You're wasting time. Hurry up!"

She winced at her mother's harsh tone. With a sigh, the girl gathered herself from the bed then dressed as she was expected—a button down shirt and skirt.

Violet knew her mother would criticize her hair if she stepped out of her bedroom as she was. Instead she gathered it back into a ponytail, securing it with an elastic band. The woman would still be critical, but she would just have to deal with it.

With one last glance back at the loathsome pastel room that her mother had forced upon her only daughter, Violet grabbed the garment bag then left.

Chapter 3

"*W*hat took you so long?"

Violet tried not to wince as the fiery red headed woman scowled at her. She stepped into the sitting room and stood with her hands clasped in front of her trying not to wince.

Her mother shook her head. "Sit! Dahlia is already here. You did bathe last night before you went to bed as I instructed?"

"Yes, Ma'am. All clean."

"Good. I will not allow you to embarrass this family. It is very important that you put on your best behavior. You need to make a good impression on the Sullivans that way your father can land that promotion." She spun around and shouted at the tall brunette who had just scampered into the room. "Dahlia! Work your magic on her. She needs to be perfect."

The younger woman lowered her brown eyes to Violet. "I'll do what I can."

The socialite leaned in close to the beautician. "I want her so gorgeous that the Sullivan boy will propose marriage to her at first sight."

"But she's only fifteen!"

"Sixteen," Violet interrupted earning a searing glare from her mother. She bowed her head, not wanting to anger the woman even further. The last time that happened Violet had received an unanticipated haircut. Her curly locks were just now brushing past her shoulders, she didn't wish for them to be chopped to jaw length ever again.

Her mother placed a hand on her daughter's shoulder and squeezed. "Then they'll be secretly engaged for two years. I don't care, just do not screw this up. Either of you!"

With those last words, the red head stormed out of the room. Dahlia winced as the door slammed shut. Several framed pictures rattled against the wall. "Mrs. Piccolo should really do something about that temper of hers…"

Violet said nothing and continued to stare straight ahead. She wanted to fight against her parents, but didn't know if she had the courage to do so. Instead she was trapped, performing like their personal marionette.

Dahlia patted the girl's hand. "It will be okay, keep your chin up. Now, let's make you beautiful."

The teenager squeezed her eyes shut wishing time would just stop so that she could find an escape from the chaotic world she was trapped in.

Chapter 4

It seemed like forever that Violet had been sitting in that horrible chair as the beautician sculpted the teenager's curls, and painted her nails and face. When she caught a glimpse of herself in the mirror looking like some sort of French courtesan she wanted to cry. Now, she really did resemble a little doll.

Just as Dahlia finished helping her get dressed, Violet's mother peeked in the room. Rather than purring her approval, she shrieked in rage. She grabbed her daughter by the arm and tore at the dress. "No, no, no! It's all wrong. She needs to be perfect, this isn't perfect!"

She stalked out of the room, leaving behind a shell-shocked beautician who remained frozen horror.

Violet moved to take off the gown when her mother burst into the room once again. Before Dahlia could protest, a garment bag was tossed into her arms. "Redo everything! She looks ridiculous!"

The door slammed behind the irate red head before anyone could think of a word to say.

"I'm sorry you have to put up with her," Violet said once they were alone again.

"I'm sorry you have to live with her." The beautician flinched then shook her head. "I apologize. I didn't mean it like that."

"No, she is difficult. Both of them are."

Dahlia nodded as she unzipped the bag. A flash of silver caught her eye. Fear transpired into pleasure at the sight of the new gown. "This is gorgeous!"

Violet suppressed a groan as the dress was removed from the bag. The silky silver material shimmered in the light. She noted it was a flowing strapless ball gown with a sweetheart neckline. The bodice was covered with sequins, its floor length skirt was full with sparkling accents scattered throughout. It looked magical. Violet's stomach turned. She felt even more ill at the sight of the ice pick strappy heels. "I'm going to break my neck in this. Of course I'll probably suffocate first."

"Nonsense. Let's get you ready that way your mother will stop breathing down both of our necks!"

Much to Violet's chagrin she found herself glued to the chair once again as her hair and makeup were redone. Dahlia went for a more dreamy style with soft colors and large romantic curls that tumbled down around Violet's creamy complexion. Afterwards she found herself squeezed into the dress. Bits of glitter fell like teardrops to the carpeted floor. She struggled to breathe as Dahlia zipped her up. Violet wiggled in discomfort. The skirt was too long to even consider wearing shorter heels. She winced as the shoes pinched her feet. It would be a pain filled evening for certain.

"You look beautiful," Dahlia gasped taking in the petite girl's glamorous appearance.

Violet gave her a tiny smile. She didn't care how she looked. She had no desire to take part in her parents' plans. All she wanted was to turn eighteen so she could be rid of their outrageous rules forever.

"It's about time!" Her mother stepped inside the room with a velvet box in her hands. She put it down on the table then looked her daughter over. "Much better. Thank you, Dahlia. I could never make this girl presentable without you."

"You're welcome, Mrs. Piccolo." The brunette gathered her things in a hurry, preparing to be dismissed. She smiled as she was handed an envelope then shooed out the door. "Best of luck, Miss Violet!"

Violet's heart sank as she found herself left alone with her controlling mother.

The woman spun her daughter around then removed a set of diamond drop earrings and a matching necklace. Once they were affixed she looked Violet over with a scrutinizing eye. "Remember not to screw any of this up. You are to keep Jared Sullivan happy no matter what. Do you understand?"

"Yes, Ma'am." Violet balled her hands into fists as she drew a sharp breath. She couldn't believe she was considering saying what she was about to next. "Do you even remember that it's my birthday?"

"It's only a day. In a few years you will conveniently forget about them."

"But sixteen is supposed to be a special age…"

"Violet, drop this nonsense. This is far more important than some stupid, immature tradition. You are not a baby anymore, so stop acting like on!"

Violet found herself dragged out of the room. From there she knew she would have to suffer through an hour wasted on photos and countless lectures on how to behave. She wanted to vomit.

Chapter 5

"*V*iolet! Are you paying attention?"

The teenaged girl shifted in discomfort as she pondered why her mother couldn't have lectured her before she had to put the gown on. She was finding her ability to breathe becoming more labored. "Yes, you have told me a million times. I understand. Don't sabotage or embarrass the family... Can we please discuss something else?"

"Don't be disrespectful!" Her mother would have slapped her if it wasn't for the fact that Dahlia had already rushed home. The woman would never be able to reapply the makeup as perfect as the beautician had.

Violet said nothing and instead rose to her feet.

"Where are you going, young lady?"

"The bathroom."

"You did not ask to be excused!" Her socialite mother snapped, displeased by her daughter's behavior.

Violet gave a mock curtsey. "May I please go before the bodice of this dress causes an accident due to the enormous amount of pressure on my bladder?"

"Violet Piccolo, you will sit back down until you learn how to show proper respect. If you act like this around the Sullivans-"

Pawn. Doll. Puppet. Bargaining Chip. Just an object to be used as they wish, nothing more. She wasn't loved. She wasn't treated like a cherished daughter. They didn't care about her, just what they could get from her. She would be better off without them. They made her feel so small.

Violet lowered her head as her thoughts swarmed her mind, blocking out the woman's bitter words. She wished her life was a dream that she could awaken from. She didn't want to be used anymore.

"You never loved me!" She bolted from the room, racing past her father's office then up the stairs. Rushing into her bedroom she slammed the door shut, locking it behind her. Her heart hammered in her chest. What had she done? She had never raised her voice to her mother before. She would pay dearly for that!

Fear consumed her as she paced the hardwood floor. She could hear her parents yell at her to open the door. Instead she dropped to her knees as she covered her ears and squeezed her eyes shut wishing she could vanish. When she reopened them a moment later she screamed.

Somehow either her gown had grown or she had shrunk. She was almost swimming in the silky material. Even worse, she was naked! Gathering her nerves, she tore pieces of the gown up then fashioned a makeshift dress with some bits of thread. If she could find a needle small enough she could probably sew something together. This would have to do instead.

Relieved to be clothed again, she glanced around then gasped. She was indeed still in her room, yet seemed to only be a few inches high! "How did this happen? What am I going to do? Am I dreaming or did I really shrink?"

Violet looked at the huge world that was her room. Everything was so big! She didn't know what to do.

She doubted her parents would be able to drag her off to her blind date now. She supposed that was a tiny something to be pleased about given her current situation.

Barefoot and wearing a drafty makeshift dress, she walked towards her desk. She hoped she would not encounter any insects or spiders. What she could once stomp on with her shoe would now pose the threat of death.

Nervous, Violet peered around. So far she didn't see anything moving in her room other than her own shadow. That was a huge relief. Now if only she could figure out what to do.

As she turned toward the bottom drawer, a large shadow loamed over her. Before she could scream, her vision filled with black.

Chapter 6

*A*mber eyes slit open as a groan passed through pink lips. Violet blinked realizing that she was no longer in a familiar place. Instead of being in a room with painted walls decorated with pictures, they were a dark textured brown.

Frowning, she sat up, leaning closer to the nearest wall. Was that… dirt? She lowered her gaze to what she thought was a bed, but discovered that it was more like a large pillow. "Where am I?"

"Calm down, dear," a sweet voice said from behind her.

Violet turned her head and screamed. Something that resembled a large field mouse stood over her. Terrified, she leaped from the bed then almost fell over. The mouse caught her arm before she could smash her face into the ground.

"Take it easy, Thumbelina."

The panic came to an abrupt end as confusion washed over her. "Thumbelina? You mean like the fairytale?"

The mouse chuckled. "That is your name, dear."

Violet pushed her strawberry blonde bangs away from her eyes. What was going on? The last thing she remembered was shrinking. She glanced down at herself then gasped as she realized that she was no longer clad in the scraps she fashioned out of her Prom dress. Instead she wore a rather simple white dress with a pink sash. "Where did this come from?"

"Don't be silly. You always wore that." The mouse touched the confused girl's forehead, "It appears your fever has gone down. Mr. Mole will be happy about that."

"Mr. Mole?"

The field mouse chuckled. "Your fiancé, dear. Don't you remember? You had gone out into the cold after the announcement and fell ill. We nursed you back to health."

Violet's mouth felt dry. "My name isn't Thumbelina. It's Violet Piccolo. I have never seen you before in my life. So, if you don't mind, I would like to leave now."

"Nonsense! You have an obligation to fulfill, and will stay right here with me until you are married!"

Chapter 7

Violet felt ill. She had gone from one control freak to another. Unlike her mother, this one could potentially give her rabies. She didn't want to date her father's, boss's son and she most certainly did not desire to marry outside of her own species! The idea of it made her feel even more nauseated.

There was only one thing she could do; find a way to escape. It was obvious that she was underground. However if she recalled the tale of Thumbelina, she should be able to find a tunnel that would lead to the surface.

"Thumbelina, are you listening?"

The girl shook her head in defiance. "I don't know who you think I am, but this is all wrong. I don't belong here. I'm human, not a mole. The best mate for a mole is another mole. Please just let me go."

The mouse narrowed her beady eyes at her. "Don't be silly. You aren't going anywhere. This is where you will live and die. There will be no changing that."

Violet squeezed her eyes shut. She had to think of a solution and fast. There had to be some way to change her fate. She couldn't figure out what to do. The last time she tried to stand up for herself she shrank. What would happen if she tried it again? Perhaps she would grow? Maybe it was like *The Adventures of Alice in Wonderland*, yet different.

You're not Alice, her mind argued. Violet drew a deep breath as she clenched her hands into fists. "Please pardon me, but the answer is still no. I am too young to marry anyone, animal and human alike. I wish to leave now."

"Didn't you hear me?" The mouse began, her sweet tone turning sour. "You are not allowed to leave here!"

Violet's heart raced. She didn't want to be trapped. She also didn't belong underground. The idea of being forced to live down there forever made her feel like vomiting. She drew back a few steps. "I am sorry, but no!"

"Thumbelina!"

She bolted away at a blind run out of the room then found herself faced with a massive collection of tunnels. She took the nearest one and continued her escape. She didn't care where she ended up as long as it was far away from the horrible mouse. How could that rodent even be able to communicate with her? Animals couldn't talk. Either way, she was tired of being controlled. Her parents doing it was one thing, but a mouse she didn't even know was ludicrous.

Violet hoped she didn't get lost in the tunnels. It was quite difficult to see where she was going. As she took a sharp turn, the ground gave way beneath her. She choked on a scream as she fell through the earth. She hoped her death would be painless.

Chapter 8

The first thing Violet noticed was a warmth that flowed around her. Curious, she opened her eyes then gasped at the sight of a giant. It looked to be female with long brown hair and green eyes. The second thing she realized was that she was lying in the giantess's hand.

"Take it easy. I won't hurt you, I promise." The person she realized looked close to her age and had a very kind voice. "Are you all right?"

Violet rose to her knees. She was still wearing the same white dress from earlier. "Yes, thank you. I don't understand what is going on. I should be close to the same size as you, yet… I'm as tall as a thumb."

A man with auburn hair and dark blue eyes leaned over the female stranger's shoulder. He pushed the muzzle of the horse he was leading away from his head. "Is she a fairy? She doesn't have any wings."

The brunette laughed. "I apologize. You must find me rude. My name is Cybele and this is Tristan. You are lucky that we were traveling through these tunnels when you fell."

"I'm Violet. Do you know why I am so small?"

"No, but I think if you search for the Crystal Garden, that you might find some answers."

The petite girl frowned. "What is that?"

"A quest you need to take. I can't tell you much more, it is, however, worth taking."

"I see." Violet lowered her head. "Not that anything makes sense anymore. I thought Thumbelina was fiction, but that's what the field mouse called me. It's just like the story, except I don't know if I'll even have a happy ending… or want one."

"Happy endings aren't guaranteed. You have to work for them." Cybele paused as she began to walk, her footsteps gentle as though she didn't want to jostle Violet. "Once we leave the tunnels I'll put you down. That will be a good start. The rest will be up to you."

"Just please don't take me to the mouse or the mole."

"We promise."

Violet didn't know why she felt relaxed accompanying the two strangers, but it was better than being trapped underground with that horrible rodent.

She felt her adrenaline rush at the sight of daylight shining through the exit. As long as the mouse didn't track her down she should remain safe… she hoped.

Once they were free of the tunnels, Cybele set her down on a rock. "This is as far as I can take you. The rest is up to you."

Violet glanced around. Rocks, long blades of grass, some wild flowers in the distance; it seemed safe enough. "Thank you."

Cybele nodded. "If you make it to the Crystal Garden, look for either me, a girl named Bianca, or another one called Lunette. We may need your help in the future."

"I'll try to remember."

"Good luck."

"You too and thank you again!" Violet gave a small wave as they departed. She turned toward the

forest then drew a deep breath. The world was so much bigger when you're only a few inches high.

Chapter 9

*V*iolet decided after a long debate to just start walking and hope she didn't come across any potential enemies. She wished Cybele would have allowed her to stay with them. It would have been much easier to avoid any danger. After all, things were far more terrifying when you were a tiny person.

At least it seemed to be a nice day out with no rain clouds in sight. The air smelled fresh. Much more so than her city condo in New York. She could see a gentle stream, trees, bushes bearing fruit, and yards of grass poking up from the soil. The sunlight felt warm reminding her that it was almost spring. She was even more delighted to see colorful flowers sprinkled around. At that moment she was reminded of Alice from *The Adventures of Alice in Wonderland* after she had eaten the side of the mushroom that made her shrink. A part of Violet would rather be the curious heroine who chased after a white rabbit rather than Thumbelina. No one tried to pair Alice with a mole.

Uncertain of where to go, she slid off the rock. It was higher than she expected. Luckily she did not hurt herself as she almost landed on her butt.

Well, if Cybele wanted her to seek out the Crystal Garden, Violet decided that looking in a field of flowers would be a good start. They didn't look too far away. She headed off at a brisk pace in their direction.

If she were her normal size it would have taken only a few steps. She didn't like being short, but this was much worse! She hoped no one was going to step on her.

After what felt like miles she finally made it to the flower patch. Violet smiled up at the colorful blossoms. She hoped, however, that these flowers would not strike up a conversation with her. Talking mice was quite enough for her. She knew she wasn't ready for plant life to speak to her as well. The aroma she noted was sweet and intense, not too overpowering which was surprising considering her size. The flowers in fact resembled trees in comparison.

What would have been tiny buttercups were the size dinner plates. Curious, she touched one of the petals and marveled at how soft they were. If she had to spend the night in the forest she would have to make a mental note to use the petals for a bed.

Violet guessed it wouldn't be too bad of a place to live. One berry might potentially be enough to feed her for a full day.

As she moved towards a small forest of daisies, she heard a rustling in the distance. She shifted her gaze around wishing she had some sort of a weapon. There was no telling what she would encounter being so tiny. A large spider could be the size of an elephant for all she knew!

That thought snapped her out of her stupor. She gathered her wits and darted back towards the buttercups, diving into the cluster. She caught a movement out of the corner of her eye. Fearful she held her breath. In silence, she waited. Nothing happened.

Determined that perhaps her nerves were getting the best of her, Violet rose to her feet. No sooner had she taken a single step did someone or something seize her from behind, and press some sort of blade to her throat.

"Move and die."

Chapter 10

"Who are you?" Violet found herself unable to keep her voice from trembling. She had never been attacked by a stranger before. The idea that every breath she drew could be her last was horrifying.

The voice which sounded masculine snorted. "Do you really expect me to give you an answer? Who do you work for?"

"No one!"

"Then how did you get here? I have never seen you before in my life."

Violet swallowed back the fear that was bubbling to her throat. "You wouldn't believe me if I told you. Listen, I'm not your enemy. All I want to do is figure out how to get back to my original size!"

"Right..."

"It's the truth." She paused, fighting to find the correct words. Deciding that it was her last shot she shared her entire story from the time she woke up that morning in her bed to the moments that led up to her attacker finding her.

"The Crystal Garden you say?" His hold on Violet didn't waver, although his voice held a tone of interest. "How do you know about that place?"

"I already told you, a girl that you might call a giantess, mentioned it." Desperate she drew a breath.

"You may do what you want with me. Just please don't kill me."

The stranger hesitated a moment then spun her around. He narrowed silver eyes at her face and dress. "You don't look like a Woodlin."

"I'm not. I don't even know what that is."

He sheathed his dagger. "Tell me the truth, what are you doing out here? It is not a safe area."

"I already told you, I'm running away from a field mouse that wants to marry me off to a mole." Violet dropped her face in her hands. "How did my life become so messed up so fast?"

"Then who are you really?"

She sighed, growing tiresome of the countless questions. "My name is Violet Piccolo. I'm usually five feet tall but somehow shrunk to the size I am right now. For whatever reason, the mouse believes I am Thumbelina. Animals aren't supposed to be able to talk!"

"You are not going to last long out here on your own."

She narrowed her eyes at the young man. He had unruly brown hair the color of fresh brewed tea. She couldn't seem to get over how striking his eyes were. They seemed to sparkle as if they had just been polished. He wore a simple slate blue tunic with dark pants and boots. She could see several sheathed daggers on his belt and strapped to his leg. "Are you some sort of hunter?"

"You are a strange one, but no, I am not."

"Then what or who are you?"

"I am not telling."

Violet fought against rolling her eyes. "Can I at least have a name or something to call you?"

He examined one of his daggers, slashed at a stalk of grass to test the blade. "Why? It's not like we will see each other again."

Her stomach turned at the idea of being left alone. "You mean you're just going to leave me here to die? Maybe there is something I can do to help."

His lips curved with interest. "Is that so? How serious are you about that Crystal Garden quest of yours?"

"What do you mean?"

"Are you planning on finding the Garden or is that all just talk."

"Why should it matter to you?"

He twirled the dagger around in his gloved hands. "Simple. If you are the Chosen of the Crystal Garden for this land then perhaps you will be of interest to me after all. You can save us from the Woodlins."

"So, you'll help me?"

"Only if you promise to end the curse. That's all I'm after— freedom."

"If it means that I can get as far away from the mouse and mole then it's a deal."

"Fine then. You can call me Zandr. Just know that if you double cross me, I will not hesitate to kill you."

Violet nodded. She hoped she had made the right decision by placing her life in the hands of such a ruffian. At least she was no longer alone.

Chapter 11

Violet winced as she stepped on something sharp. Trailing after Zandr barefoot had to be one of the most painful things she had ever done. She rarely went anywhere barefoot.

"Keep up," the brunette man ordered from a few feet in front of her. His hair fluttered around his face in uneven tufts. He would look handsome if he didn't scowl so much.

"Ow!" she yelped again as something unseen threatened to impale her sole.

Zandr came to a halt then approached her. "I should have known traveling this way would be a waste of time. It'll be dangerous, but take out your wings."

Violet blinked. "My wings?"

He sighed in impatience. "Yes, we'll fly instead."

"You mean… are you a fairy?"

"… You're not?"

"No, I am human. Or at least was."

Zandr groaned, pressing a hand to his face. "So, you cannot fly… great. I'm guessing you can't make yourself bigger either."

"No, otherwise I wouldn't be in this mess!" She paused as a thought struck her. "Wait. Can you?"

"Long story, but no. Not anymore." He rubbed his face as he began to pace. "You are ill suited to be traveling anywhere dressed like that."

Violet folded her arms over her chest in frustration. "I didn't plan this."

"We need to at least get you some shoes. I probably won't be able to carry you for too long… This is quite troublesome."

"I'm fine with whatever ideas you come up with."

Zandr frowned at Violet's bare feet. "As you are currently attired you will only slow us down. I can't fly too far if I carry you, so I'll just have to do it on foot."

Violet let out a gasp when without warning he scooped her up into his arms. She could feel a blush warm her cheeks. She had never been so close to a guy before. It made her feel very self-conscious. "So, where are you taking me?"

"Someplace to find you some better clothing." He adjusted her a bit then began walking. "You're lucky that you don't seem to weigh too much. This may not be as bad as I was anticipating."

"You have my mother to thank for that. She kept me on a strict diet." Violet's voice softened as she reflected back, "Everything in my life was regulated just so. I could never do whatever I wanted to. I was always so jealous of my classmates who had normal families that loved them."

"What was wrong with yours?"

"They didn't care about me. Neither of them. My father let my mother control me to her heart's content. I wouldn't have minded if she showed me a shred of affection. Instead she'd either scream at me or flat out ignore me. I was never good enough. Never will be."

Zandr fell silent a moment, but didn't stop.

Violet picked at her nails then bowed her head. "I apologize. I shouldn't have shared such personal information. That was very rude of me for complaining like that."

"How would your mother have reacted if she had overheard you?" He inquired.

"I would have gotten yelled at then banished to my room. She would have called me a disgrace and an ungrateful little brat. I can't wait until I turn eighteen. Then I can leave forever."

"Why?"

"That's the age that identifies someone as an adult. At least where I'm from," she added after realizing that he wasn't familiar with human laws or terms.

"I see."

Violet fought the urge to squirm. She hated small talk. It was something her mother forced her to do a lot of with strangers. She wondered if her mother would approve of her only daughter being carried in the arms of a fairy. Probably not. The thought of the woman's outrage made her flinch. "So, is the age of adulthood different for fairies? Are your life spans longer than say one hundred?"

"You talk too much."

"Well, you don't talk enough," she replied feeling a bit lame.

Zandr shook his head. "I talk an adequate amount. You, however, don't seem to know when to stop."

Violet bit her tongue. It was best not to argue. If he preferred silence then so be it. As long as he helped her that was what was most important. Instead she looked at the life growing around them. A small smile spread over her lips. She loved looking at flowers no matter her size. "I always wanted to have a garden of my own, but my mother frowned upon the idea of me playing in the dirt as she called it. A lady should never

get filthy so that dream was always dashed. I did it again. I'm sorry. I'll stop talking now."

"I didn't say that."

"But you-"

"I said you talk too much, not that you cannot talk. It is obvious that you are uneasy." He sighed. "You can relax. I already know a bit about you."

Chapter 12

"How much?" Violet's mind whirled from the confession. "And please don't tell me that I am Thumbelina. That's just absurd."

"You mentioned Cybele. She is one of the Chosen of the Crystal Garden. She had returned peace to her land a few months ago. She would only suggest the quest if you too, are one of the chosen. This means you can return order to our land."

"What else do you know of me?"

Zandr shrugged. "Not much. However we have been looking for you. That is part of the reason why I found you. It was written in the prophecy. 'A flightless fairy that suggests she is a human made smaller' or something like that."

"There's a prophecy about Thumbelina?"

"Yes."

Violet frowned. That was never mentioned in the fairytale. Then again, Thumbelina didn't shrink as she had. She had been small to begin with. "So… fairytales are real?"

Zandr's dark brows knitted together. "We don't have tails. Only wings."

"I meant tales as in stories."

"I still do not understand what you mean."

She wanted to hide her face. Instead she squeezed her eyes shut. "Forget it. Translation errors…"

"What is that?"

"Don't worry about it. It's just my odd human speech." Violet decided she might be better off just shutting up before she confused them both. Of course she guessed the damage may already be done. At least Zandr didn't seem too annoyed and just dumped her off leaving her to fend for herself. Her mind flitted back to their first encounter. "Wait, if you need me then why did you say you would kill me if I double crossed you?"

"Simple. I do not know you. You may be the Chosen One, however, that doesn't mean you are trustworthy. I have no proof that the Crystal Garden actually exists, but if it will save our land, I'll put my faith in it."

"I see. So even though we are working together we are at odds?"

"Our goals are not the same."

Violet flinched. Perhaps things were more complicated than she had anticipated. Just as she opened her mouth to reply, a high pitched laughter erupted from behind the pair.

Zandr swung around in warning. He withdrew one of his daggers as he set Violet down behind him. "Reveal yourself!"

Violet gasped as the field mouse emerged from under some brush. "Oh no... please no."

The mouse showed her teeth then hissed. "I shall take back what is mine now, thank you very much."

Chapter 13

*V*iolet stared in horror as the rodent barred her fangs and leapt towards the fairy, swiping at him with one paw.

Zandr dodged, slashing out with his blade as he shielded Violet with his body. He winced as a claw raked against his arm. "You can't have her, you beast!"

The mouse cackled. "If you give her to me, I might allow you to live."

"Never! She has a higher duty than marrying your friend." Zandr struck out again, slicing the rodent's tail in the process.

She gave a shrill squeak. "What little you know of any of us. One way or another she will be mine again. Don't ever forget that. I'll have my eye on you."

Before Violet could blink the mouse scampered off. The teenaged girl collapsed to her knees clutching her chest as her heart hammered from the adrenaline. "I don't understand why she wants me so much. Doesn't she know of any female moles that she can marry off?"

Zandr wiped his bloodstained dagger on the ground. "Perhaps there is more to her desires for you than you may assume. There may be an entirely different reason all together."

"That could be." Violet lifted her head to the fairy then winced as her amber gaze fell upon his injured forearm. "She hurt you."

"It's just a scratch. I'll be fine."

"I thought only rats were vicious."

Zandr helped her up. "Any living thing has the potential to cause damage if provoked. However she was no ordinary mouse."

"Why do you say that?"

"She could speak. Unless the curse had just recently granted the animals the ability to talk like us, there is something unusual about her. I'd keep my distance if I were you."

Violet whirled around. "Wait, I mentioned that the mouse could speak earlier and you didn't comment on it. Why?"

He shrugged. "I needed to see it with my own eyes."

"To make sure I'm not crazy?"

"Yes, I don't know you. You could have been delirious at that time." He scowled at the direction the mouse had fled. "We can argue about this later. It would be best if we get away from here. She might find reinforcements."

Before Violet could give a response Zandr lifted her into his arms and rather than take off at a run, shimmery silver wings formed on his back. She stared in amazement as they took to the sky.

Chapter 14

They had only traveled a short distance before Zandr had to land. He sat on the ground trying to catch his breath. "You may not weigh that much, but I still cannot fly too far with you. At least I should have gotten us far enough away from that mouse to delay another attack."

Violet twisted a lock of hair around her fingers. She wished they could have continued gliding through the air. The ability to fly was something she always wished she could have. She loved the feel of the wind in her hair. Just the idea of it was freeing. However, she didn't want Zandr to hurt himself so she refrained from pressing him to continue. "You didn't have to strain yourself. Walking would have been fine."

Zandr shook his head. "I'm not unqualified as a warrior, however, I did not wish to tempt fate and allow that rodent to return with her allies. More than likely, they would have kidnapped you as I was engaged in battle."

She couldn't help but smile. He had put her safety first despite the fact that he could have injured himself while flying with her. "You would have fared better than me. I have no fighting abilities."

His brow creased. "You have never held a weapon before in your life?"

"Not really," Violet chewed on her bottom lip as she reconsidered. "I did do archery in school, but that was only for a week before we switched to softball."

"A soft….ball?"

"It's a game that might be a little too complicated to explain."

"Very well," the fairy said, though his face still held a puzzled expression. "So, you have used a bow and arrow before?"

Violet nodded feeling a bit flustered. "I'm not very good though. I could never hit the center of the bull's eye."

"Well, that's something at least." Zandr walked towards what Violet guessed were tiny twigs or perhaps straw if she had been her normal size. He picked up a long one then with his dagger, carved holes at the end. Then he took out what looked like floss from his pouch tying it at both ends.

"You made a bow?"

"Not my best work and if you aren't careful it will probably break. However this way you won't be as defenseless."

She scowled at the makeshift weapon. "Don't I need arrows?"

"Way ahead of you." With a swift movement her sliced several pieces of reed into long sticks then notched them on one end. "They are not the best, but should cause some damage if you fire them well enough. You'll have to hold onto them until we get you to a town."

Violet examined her new weapon for a brief moment. She didn't know how useful it would be. She might have been better off with a stick. "It's better than nothing I suppose. Thank you."

He nodded. "Let's continue on. Will you be all right with walking for a while?"

Violet took a few testing steps. To her delight, her feet didn't hurt. "The ground seems softer here. I should be fine."

"Good. Then let us be off."

Chapter 15

Violet ran her fingers over the bow. She appreciated Zandr's gesture in making it for her, especially since he had been rather unpleasant since they first met. However a part of her questioned if she could even use it. It had been at least a year since she had a week's worth of archery. Bows were not very easy to use. It took a lot of coordination and strength to properly shoot an arrow. Hers often fell short of the target or flew past it. Now that she was expected to use her skills as a means to protect herself—she felt quite incompetent.

"You're rather quiet," her traveling companion remarked.

She felt herself flush. "I guess I'm just nervous. I have never fought anyone before in my life. Plus, like I said earlier, I'm not very good with a bow."

"You have no experience with any other weapons?"

"Well, no-"

"Then that is your best chance to survive."

Violet continued trailing after Zandr. At least she was no longer stabbing her feet as she walked. She didn't realize that they were in one of the wild flower patches until she looked up. Soft petals of various colors were all around her. She smiled at the sweet fragrance. If she were her normal size she might have picked them and put them in her hair. Now she could use them as a bed.

"Keep up. You don't want to chance an encounter with a bee."

She gasped in horror at that thought. She didn't like bees. The fact that they were probably much bigger than her made it even worse. With that thought in mind, she trotted after Zandr.

"Calm down. They will not attack unless provoked."

"But you said-"

"Stay away from the flowers and they won't become angry. It's as simple as that."

Violet frowned. "I'm not a threat to them. I don't even have wings!"

"You still resemble a fairy."

"You mean fairies take nectar?"

Zandr gave her a slow nod. "It's a good food source. At least for now."

"You're not telling me something."

"It'll be easier to show you. Besides, we're almost there."

Violet scowled, but continued to follow Zandr. Her mind puzzled around what he could be leaving out. By the time they came to a halt she still didn't have an answer to her own question.

"We're here."

She lifted her head then felt her jaw drop at the sight of the town. From first glance it looked normal with food stalls, shops, and a pub. Then she noticed how small the people were in comparison. "It's-it's... human. I mean the town is. Why would fairies live in a town so much bigger than they were?"

Zandr gave her a bitter smile. "This is why I need you to break the curse. We can't change our size as long as it is in existence."

Chapter 16

"Wait...so are you saying that you can normally change your size?"

"That's why we have the ability to hide our wings, so we can walk amongst humans. We prefer being human-sized because it makes things like trading and work much easier," Zandr explained. "However, being small and living in a human-sized village is quite inconvenient. We've had to come up with alternate methods to get by with everyday life. It has not been easy. You have only been that size for less than a day. We have been this way for years."

Violet's amber gaze shifted from her companion to the fairies flitting about. Some had to work in a team to slice apart some berries. A few men clustered together in an effort to craft weapons. Several women were cutting apart a long dress as others were sewing the scraps into clothing. Violet felt the guilt over her earlier complaints rise to her chest. "I'm sorry. I can't make any promises since I don't know how I am supposed to break the curse, but I will do what I can."

"That will have to be enough… for now." Zandr turned back towards the street. "Come along. Let's get you some shoes."

Violet followed without protest. She was too absorbed in looking at what the residents of the town had to resort to in order to survive. It seemed like a lot of them had cannibalized their own belongings, taking the materials to make small versions. From the tavern she could see that the large steins had been exchanged for thimbles. "Do you also live here?"

"Sometimes." Zandr led her towards what she guessed was a cobbler shop. Inside were a few rows of leather shoes, more than likely made from human sized boots. A scrawny red headed boy rushed up to him. "Ash, I need a pair of shoes for her. Can you or your father be of any assistance?"

"Certainly! Father, the prince is here!"

Violet's eyes widened in shock at her traveling companion. "You're a prince?"

"Yes."

"You never told me!"

He shrugged. "You never asked."

A graying man emerged from the back. He grinned at the sight of Zandr then bowed his head. "Good to see you, Your Highness. What can I do for you today?"

"I need shoes for her," he gestured to Violet. "Can you help?"

The man scratched his head. "Please step forward, dear, so I can see your feet."

Violet felt heat rise to her cheeks as she did as he wished. She felt foolish standing there as the cobbler took her right foot in his hands.

He smiled with a slight nod. "I think I have just the pair. I imagine you might be walking a good distance."

Zandr spoke up before Violet could reply. "She's going on the quest for the Crystal Garden."

"So, she is indeed the flightless one that we have been waiting for. In that case…" The man disappeared behind a box midsentence then emerged with what appeared to be a pair of sandals in hand. "These should do nicely. Light, yet sturdy. Perfect for long distances."

Violet accepted the shoes then slipped them on. She took a few experimental steps then lifted her brows in wonder. "These have to be the best shoes I have ever worn! They're a bit springy, yet firm."

"Call them a gift. After all if you are to save us, you should have proper footwear."

Zandr's eyebrows lifted. "Are you certain? I may not have much on me, but-"

"Nonsense. She is our savior and should be treated as such. It is the least I can do. Now go to the tavern and have some of the wonderful acorn stew my wife has cooked up. She will be pleased to see you."

Violet winced as her stomach grumbled at the mentioning of food. "It might be a good idea to eat something before we set out… wherever it is we need to go."

"Fine," the prince sighed. He turned back to the cobbler then bowed his head. "Thank you again, Rovynn."

"Thank you," Violet smiled at the man and his son as she departed with Zandr. To her relief, they were headed towards the tavern. She could smell something mouth-watering wafting in the air. "I have never had acorn stew before. Is it any good?"

"It is what it is. Come along."

The inside of the place smelled even better. Zandr sidled up to the bar. A pretty middle aged woman grinned as she approached. She gave him a brief curtsy. "If it isn't my favorite prince. Your Highness. Can I interest you in a bowl of my finest? It's even better than it was last time you had it."

"Two please." He motioned for Violet to take the seat next to him.

The woman beamed at the insecure teen-aged girl. "Hello there. You must be his number two. Zandr here doesn't normally have any companions with him. My, you are a pretty one…"

"Fern…" he said shifting in his seat with slight discomfort. "The food, please?"

"Right away, Your Majesty." She gave Violet a wink before dashing off.

Zandr released a sigh of what had to have been relief.

Violet perched herself on what looked to have been an empty spool of thread. It wasn't very comfortable even with the pillow attached to the top as a cushion. "Is she the cobbler's wife?"

"Yes. She's nosy too, so be careful with what you say."

"I see." Violet perked up when a fresh thimble of water and some bread was placed in front of them. She took a generous gulp then another until it was all gone. "Wow! I must have been thirstier than I thought."

"She'll bring another soon." Zandr took a bite of one of the pieces of bread then flinched. "Bread is still as hard as a rock. She must not have found the right ratio of time to bake it yet."

"It should soften a bit in the stew though."

"You are probably right."

Violet hesitated a moment then asked the question that had been racing through her mind. "So, why didn't you tell me who you are?"

"It's not that important— at least not anymore. It's not like I'll get the kingdom when I come of age. Not with five older siblings. Plus with our current situation… it's best not to advertise."

"The Woodlins."

"Among other enemies."

Violet opened her mouth to ask for more information, but their food had arrived. Happy at being able to eat at last, she took the wooden spoon that she guessed had been hand carved and dug in. It was warm and a bit spicy—completely unlike what she had been anticipating.

"Fern has improved the recipe," Zandr remarked after sampling his own.

"I told you," the barmaid laughed as she refilled Violet's cup.

Just as Violet almost finished her bowl, a loud sound that resembled a bell rang through the air.

Zandr cursed, dropping his spoon. "They would attack now of all times!"

"Who?" The strawberry blonde squeaked out, alarmed at the idea of engaging in a battle.

"The Woodlins."

Chapter 17

Violet raced out of the tavern chasing after Zandr. There was panic in the streets as some of the townspeople fled in one direction while others rushed in the other with weapons in hand. In the distance she could see what looked like faeries dressed in leaves with rough scaly skin that resembled tree bark.

"Great. They brought their queen…" the fairy prince growled as a feminine looking one wearing a skimpy gown the color of dirty copper pennies marched to the front of the group. Her dark lips smirked in pleasure at the sight of Violet, standing a few inches away from Zandr.

"My, my. Look at what the cat dragged in. I didn't expect you to make it this far… I'm impressed," the queen cackled, twirling her whip with one hand while fingering a dark lock of hair with the other. "This might be entertaining."

"What is your purpose here?" The prince growled, his voice edged with fury. "We have stayed off your lands. That was the deal, yet you still attack us."

The Woodlin Queen smiled. "Simple. You have something that we want."

Zandr narrowed his silver eyes at her. "What pray tell?"

"Her." A dark painted finger pointed to Violet.

"Me?" The girl gasped in shock. "Why does everyone want me? I'm no one important."

"Oh, what little you know, girl. You are a prize worth killing for."

"You can't have her," the prince hissed sliding in front of Violet, in a protective gesture.

"Then you leave me no choice." The queen struck her whip out, hitting Zandr, forcing him to the side. The next strike snared Violet before she could react.

A scream escaped the girl's throat as she was yanked towards the woman. The queen grabbed Violet by the hair then signaled for her army to attack.

"No!" Zandr pushed himself to his feet as Violet struggled against her captor.

"Let me go!" The strawberry blonde teenager yelled, helpless to defend herself. She couldn't fire a bow let alone slash out with an arrow with her arms bound to her sides. She could feel the coarse leather slicing into her skin with each movement.

"The more you resist, the more you will bleed," the queen smirked as her guards grabbed the frightened girl. "Say goodbye to your prince. You won't ever see him or daylight ever again."

Before Violet could make another sound, a sharp pain flooded her skull as everything went black.

Chapter 18

"Where am I?" Violet frowned at finding herself in what seemed to be a cloud of fog. She turned in hopes of finding something to verify her location, but everything was covered in the thick white mist.

"Do not despair," a soft voice whispered.

"Who are you? Where are you?" The petite girl backed up a few steps in fear. She didn't like being unable to see what was around her. It was rather unnerving.

"I won't harm you." A figure emerged from in front of her. To Violet's surprise, it was a blonde girl with sad violet eyes wearing a lavender dress. "You're safe, for now at least."

"Where am I?"

The girl's curls bounced as she shook her head. "It's hard to explain. At the moment, you are unconscious. It is imperative that you escape once you awaken. I cannot aid you too much, at least for now. It's draining just talking to you. However, you must continue your search for the Crystal Garden. If you don't… There's a lot at stake."

Violet scowled. She hated having secrets kept from her, especially when she had no clue what she was supposed to do. "I still don't understand what is going on. It's so confusing."

"Spells do that. I should know; I was hit with an ugly one. The important thing is to distinguish truth from fiction and fight for what you want most. Don't let anyone stop you, no matter what."

"How do I find the Crystal Garden?"

"That is for you to discover."

"Why can't you give me a straight answer? How can I break a curse if I don't know what I'm supposed to do?"

The girl gave her a sad smile. "Time is almost up. Now you must break free and fly."

Before Violet could ask anything more her vision filled with white as everything vanished.

Chapter 19

*V*iolet's eyes drifted open. Wherever she was, it was dark. She couldn't seem to remember much in the way anything. Her head was pounding and her limbs hurt. She tried to lift one arm, but it refused to move. Was she tied up? She seemed to be leaned against something in a sitting position. How she got there, she had no clue. She just wished all the pain would go away. If it got any worse, she might get sick.

"So, you're awake at last."

Amber eyes lifted to meet deep onyx. Violet stared with a blank expression then gasped as her mind shoved the last moments before she fell unconscious back at her. She had been kidnapped by the Woodlin Queen. The fairies. Were they okay or were they... Zandr— the thought of him being dead made her stomach twist into knots. She felt as though she were about to suffocate. She had to get free somehow! "What do you want with me?"

The Woodlin Queen laughed. "I am not a fool, little one. I will not give you the upper hand by sharing all my secrets."

"I am not a fairy, if that is what you think."

"This has nothing to do with those insolent creatures and their mockery of a monarch."

"Then why did you kidnap me?"

The queen laughed again as she walked away from the confused girl.

Violet wiggled, trying to see what she was tied to. If she could guess it might be a thick tree trunk. She winced as the ropes bit into her arms from the movement. She wondered how far away she might be from the fairy village. If only she had a dagger or something else sharp, she could use it to free herself.

She thudded the back of her head back against the tree. This was pathetic. How was she expected to do anything in this state? She didn't want to be some weakling that needed to be rescued! Unfortunately she was powerless to do anything about her horrible situation.

How did she get in this situation to begin with? She shrank, but was it all a dream? Fairies and talking animals were all fantasy. It didn't make sense for them to exist... wherever she was. The most important thing, however, was finding a way to free herself.

Violet froze as she heard movement from behind her. She squeezed her eyes shut, afraid that the queen had sent someone to kill her. Instead of feeling pain, her bounds were loosened. "What-"

"Shh! If you value your life." A deep voice warned.

She waited until the ropes fell away then turned and gasped at the sight of her rescuer. Her mind immediately flipped back to the tale of Thumbelina and the first suitor. "You're a toad!"

"Do not be rude. I'm a frog," he croaked. "Run, unless you want the queen to catch you again."

Violet rose to her feet then realizing that she had no other choice, bolted off after the amphibian.

Chapter 20

*O*nce they were far enough away, Violet and the mysterious frog came to a halt near a small pond. They each sipped at the water until they had their fill.

"You're not expecting me to marry you for saving me are you?" Violet inquired, feeling quite nervous at the concept.

"That wasn't my plan. Besides, you're not my type." He turned away from the confused girl. "If you follow the pond down from here you should be able to find the fairy village. Or should I say, what's left of it."

"What do you mean? It was destroyed?"

The frog sighed. "The Woodlins are not what you might think they are. You need to be careful though. Once you find the Crystal Garden you should be able to fix things. Until then, you will have to watch your back."

Violet blinked in surprise. "How do you know about the Crystal Garden?"

"Let's just say you remind me a bit of someone I lost. Perhaps if you win, she might get a second chance or so I hope. I must go now, so I bid you a farewell. Stay safe."

With that, the frog hopped away leaving Violet behind. She was still bewildered by the fact that she had just been rescued by a frog. At least he didn't propose marriage.

She glanced at the direction he had indicated. She supposed she had no choice, but to return to the fairy village. There was nowhere else for her to go. Plus, she didn't know how to go back home, if that was even possible.

Violet drew a breath and headed off. She hoped everyone was all right. There was no telling what might have happened after she blacked out. Just the thought of everyone she had met being dead made her heart hurt. She gripped the skirt of her white dress as she quickened her pace. "Please be okay."

Chapter 21

It had taken some time, but Violet had managed to follow the frog's instructions. What she discovered upon stepping into the fairy village made her want to cry out in pain. There was smoke all around. She could see dark stains splattered on the soil. Shreds of cloth wafted in the wind. There was no sign of life anywhere she looked. Without thinking she took off at a sprint in an effort to find any survivors.

The first place she stopped at was the tavern. Violet felt dismay to discover that it was empty. To keep from panicking she had to reassure herself that perhaps Fern was elsewhere tending to the wounded. The kind-hearted woman was not dead. She couldn't be. Neither could her husband and son. They weren't dead. Violet refused to accept any other possibility.

A little ways down she came across the cobbler's shop. It too was empty. Shoes and materials were scattered about. A sickness stirred in Violet's belly when she noticed smears of blood along the walls and floor.

She sped up her pace. Was there a hospital? Could that be where everyone was at? Perhaps they had fled the village? That thought terrified her. She didn't want to be left alone and defenseless.

She walked with caution past several more shops. Her heart leaped at finding each one empty. It was like being in a ghost town. What had once been bustling with activity was now void of all life. It brought chills down her spine.

Violet blew her bangs from her eyes. She listened for any movement, but all was silent. All she could hear were her own footsteps. It was eerie. What if there was no one left? What would she do? She didn't know the first thing about being as tiny as she was. She felt vulnerable.

"This wasn't in the story either," she muttered to herself recalling the tale of the girl everyone seemed to believe she was. Then she thought of Zandr. Did the Woodlins… she couldn't complete her thought. The notion of it was too horrible to even consider.

A gasp escaped her throat as she saw movement out of the corner of her eye. She spun around wishing she had a weapon. "Please be friend and not foe."

"Thumbelina? Is that you?" A familiar face framed by dark hair appeared from the shadows of a general store.

"Zandr… you're alive!" Before Violet could stop herself, she raced towards him throwing her arms around his torso. Tears flooded her eyes as she clung to him. "You really are alive!"

"Yes, I am." He replied his voice tinged with unease. "Can you… let go now?"

"Oh, sorry!" She stepped back, her face red with embarrassment. "I don't know what came over me. I saw the town and thought the worst… What happened here?"

"The Woodlins. How did you get back? I thought we would never see you again."

"I don't know how it's possible, but a frog saved me. How is everyone? The Woodlins didn't actually kill them, right?" Violet stepped back then blinked in surprise to see Zandr clad in all black. It took a moment before she realized that his clothing was covered in soot. Smudges of it were on her dress as well. "Were you here when the fire started?"

He nodded. "I was doing my best to rescue whoever needed help escaping from the blaze. A few didn't make it though."

"Oh," her head sank with the news. "Are Fern and her family okay?"

"Yes, they are fine." The fairy prince wiped at his face then sighed. "I guess I'll be stuck like this for a while. All the clothing and most of the weapons are gone. They were swallowed by the flames. The food too."

"What are you going to do?"

"Make the most of what we have I guess."

Violet chewed on her bottom lip a moment. "Is there anything I can do?"

"As much as I hate to ask, do you mind accompanying me back to my home?"

"You mean the castle?" She choked. That was the last place she expected to set foot in.

"Yes. There I can explain what happened to these people and ask for aid. They may not survive too long here in the trees. The town was the best shelter until now."

"I suppose, but why do you need me?"

"Someone there may have information on the Crystal Garden and the curse."

Violet's eyes brightened. 'Really? Then that's good news!"

"I have to warn you, it will not be easy to get there at our size. Even in the air we will be at risk. Being human-sized made the journey much easier."

"I see. But if what you're saying is true then we have no choice. I don't want to be cold hearted towards a lot of innocent people. I will go with you."

"Thank you." He nodded then paused. "Before we go I need to retrieve something— for you."

"Me?"

The fairy prince nodded as he dashed to what was left of the weapon-smith's shop. He dug through the rubble until he came to a long silver box. Using a key he pulled out of his waist pouch, he unlocked it.

Violet peered over his shoulder as he lifted the lid then gasped. Inside was a silver short bow with a matching quiver filled with dozens of arrows. Each had an ornate design that took her breath away. "They're beautiful. Are they worth a lot?"

Zandr smiled as he handed the weapons to her. "They are yours."

"Mine?"

"They were made specifically for the one that can free us— or so Lans, the weapon-smith insisted."

Violet realized that arguing would be futile so she slid the strap of the quiver over her shoulder as she accepted the gift. Now she would have to do anything in her power to help the fairies; it would be inconsiderate to refuse considering how much they had done for her.

"If you are ready we'll head off."

Violet nodded then found herself lifted into the fairy prince's arms and whisked off.

Chapter 22

$\mathcal{Z}$andr had only been able to travel a short distance by air before they found themselves hiking through the thick jungle like grass yet again. Violet studied him a moment in silence before remarking, "You don't seem too pleased at the idea of returning."

He stared at her for a moment. "I'm not of value to them. I am just another son with no true destiny. My two eldest brothers are more important."

"I'm sorry. I didn't mean to bring up something that was painful to you." She replied, annoyed at herself for speaking before thinking. "If it helps I don't like my family much either. They only seem to care about making me into whatever they want without considering what I might desire. I'm just a doll to them."

"Mine are actually the complete opposite." Zandr admitted. "My parents never paid much attention to me. It's not as though I'll ever become a successor to the throne. They pretty much let me do whatever I wish."

Violet narrowed her gaze as flashes of images sparked to life then diminished before she could focus on any particular one. She pressed a hand to her face as she groaned. "I don't remember mine or know if I ever had any family. I seem to have conflicting memories that don't make much sense."

Zandr stopped dead. "But you just said-"

"I don't remember." She frowned as confusion washed over her. "Everything is foggy. It's strange."

He stared in bewilderment at her before nodding his head. "The sooner we find the Crystal Garden, the better off you should be."

"I hope you are right. My head is starting to hurt." Violet felt nervous. What if the Woodlins had poisoned her? She could be dying at that very moment and would have no idea what would cure her. The thought was troubling.

Zandr quickened his pace. "Let's hurry. I don't want to risk you collapsing."

Violet didn't argue as the fairy prince pulled her along. Her mind was too wrapped around what was wrong with her. She hoped that whatever was wrong with her wasn't fatal. She didn't want to give up on her quest.

Chapter 23

*I*t was strange how different distances were when one was so small, Violet realized. What should have taken a few minutes would potentially take hours to reach. She ran her fingernails over the smooth metal of her bow. At least she had a way to fight back if they were attacked again. Of course, she hoped she wouldn't have to test her skills so soon. With her luck, the arrow would do a nosedive into the soft earth.

"Stay sharp. This area has been known to be dangerous to take on foot," Zandr warned, drawing a dagger from its sheath.

"Can we not fly over it?"

He shook his head. "It's too far to cross with you in tow. Plus, I have yet to regain my full strength."

"Great." Violet took an arrow out of her quiver, readying her bow. She prayed she wouldn't hit Zandr by accident if they did have to fight. That would be rather embarrassing.

"Stay calm and try not to shoot me."

She frowned at him. Did he just read her mind? "Clairvoyance isn't a skill of the fairies is it?"

"No why?"

"You said what I was thinking."

The prince frowned. "Odd. Well, at least I know that you will be doing your best to avoid striking me."

"Hey! It's not like I just painted a bull's eye on your back. I warned you earlier that I don't have much experience with archery, let alone shooting moving targets." Violet glared at him.

"Easy. I did not mean it as an insult."

"Well, you failed-"

Zandr covered her mouth with his free hand interrupting the beginning of her tirade. "Shh. I think something is tracking us."

Violet's eyes widened with horror at the warning. She obeyed his order, readying her bow in the direction he indicated.

Her hands shook as she notched the arrow to the string. She hoped that she was a better shot than she used to be in high school gym class.

Violent thrashing of the long blades of grass soon followed. As the pair stood in wait, a large, furry, brown spider burst through the foliage and charged.

Chapter 24

Violet choked on a scream at the size of the arachnid. It had to be as big as an elephant! The pinchers moved with menacing intent. She trembled in fear. She hated spiders. This was even worse. Before she could react, Zandr shoved her out of the way.

"Wake up and shoot!" He threw a dagger at it, but missed.

"But it's a huge spider!"

"That shouldn't make any difference. Unless you want to be its next meal— attack!"

"Right…" She picked herself back up from the ground, drew back on the line of her bow and fired the arrow striking it in one of the many legs. Violet cringed. This was a nightmare come to life.

Howling it, charged again. The fairy prince took to the air, snatching Violet up just in time.

"I don't understand. We didn't pass any webs."

Zandr set her back down. "It's a hunter."

The word wolf spider popped into her mind as she shot off another arrow. "Is it poisonous?"

"If it bites you, yes. They all secrete venom."

Violet narrowed her gaze swallowing back her terror. Two of the bulging eyes were huge. Perhaps that would be their best chance. She fired another arrow, aiming for one of the large eyes. It was a perfect shot. The arachnid squealed in pain.

Zandr must have realized what she was up to because he flew to the spider then landed on its back. He leaned forward before driving the blade of one of his daggers into the other large eye.

The spider thrashed, struggling to buck the fairy off. It's fighting, however, was in vain as Zandr slashed through its abdomen. Green ooze gushed out and soon the spider collapsed in a heap.

Violet stared in shock at the prince's handiwork as he leapt off the corpse. "You gutted it."

"I was never the type to sit around the castle trying to look important," he smirked, wiping the blood off his weapons. "Maybe it was best that I was the last born after all. My elder brothers were never very good warriors. They were better suited strategizing and handling inquiries. I guess you could say they are better leaders."

"That doesn't make you any less of a prince or a son."

He shook his head. "Warriors are made. Leaders are born. There's a million who can fight just as well if not better than me. This is where I belong. Not in that stuffy old castle."

"Even so, you aren't less than your brothers."

"Let's move on. I need to regain more strength if I'm to get you up to the castle." With that Zandr marched off, leaving Violet to race after him.

Chapter 25

*V*iolet tried to refrain from speaking. It seemed all she did was say the wrong thing without meaning to. If only she could remember things. It was so frustrating when her mind didn't seem to want to cooperate with her.

Needing a new focus, she instead turned her attention to her surroundings. The large forest was bright and colorful. Every so often she got a wider view as Zandr picked her up, flying them a short distance before setting them back down.

"What is it like to fly?" She thought out loud.

He blinked at her, shrugged. "It's hard to describe since I have done it for so long. I guess you could say it's like taking a long jump, but you can go further and higher. I never thought of it before to be honest."

"Oh. I always wondered how it felt." She paused, frowning as she tried to retrieve her memories. Nothing. "At least I thought I did. Did I get hit on the head or something? Maybe I have a concussion."

"I do not have an answer to that since I don't know what happened after you were captured by the Woodlins."

Violet pursed her lips as she walked alongside the fairy prince. "I wonder if they poisoned me or something. Is there anything that can cause... well, whatever is happening to me?"

"I cannot provide an answer to that question either."

"Great. Sorry, I'm probably stressing out over nothing. It's just… nothing like this has ever happened to me before."

He gave her a sympathetic smile. "Keep going and don't stop. That is all you can do until we figure things out. Don't ever give up."

Violet brushed a strawberry blonde curl from her face. "Thanks for the pep talk. I wish it could provide more than just a hint of comfort."

"You're scared and frustrated. It's understandable," he commented.

She frowned as a revelation hit her. "You're talking more."

"So?"

You barely said anything when we first met."

He paused as though contemplating her words. "I suppose, I have become accustomed to you. Plus, you seem more comfortable this way than traveling in complete silence."

Violet laughed. "I have no memories to escape to and my thoughts don't provide any reassurance. I'm lost in a strange land where my mind is failing me. It's rather distressing."

"Stay focused on the goal at hand. That's the best advice I can give you. Things aren't always easy."

"My life has never been easy!" she snapped. Her eyes widened in bewilderment at her harsh tone. "Oh my… I'm so sorry. I didn't mean-"

Zandr came to a halt then studied her face. "I don't think your memories are gone. It's evident that I had just struck a nerve. That's a good thing."

"So are you going to try to make me mad in hopes of jarring something loose now?"

"No, however if my guess is right, something is blocking out portions. Whether they are significant or not is unknown, but this is good news.

"What do you mean?"

"We may have a better chance of getting you back to normal."

Chapter 26

"How?" This was the first bit of good news that Violet had heard all day. Her pulse rushed at the idea of being free from the torment her mind had undergone.

"I have no idea, but we shall figure out something."

Her smile had crestfallen at his confession. She wished they could find the answer soon. Instead they continued their hike. Violet waited as Zandr made his way across the dam, then held out a hand to help her over it. She accepted, tightening her grip as her feet skidded on the wet stones.

"Are you all right?" Zandr inquired once they had cleared the stream.

Violet ran her fingers over her bow. "I just want some real answers. I'm tired of being a puppet!"

"Your parents?"

"No, I only had a mother and she was much bigger than me." The laughter that started to bubble burst as confusion took over. "Why did I say that? It can't be true."

Zandr paused in thought before speaking. "It sounds like your mind is at war. It's fighting to distinguish the real memories from the false ones. That might explain why everything is so scattered right now."

"I hope so. This is enough to drive me mad."

"Take it slow and trust yourself. Only then can you free your mind."

"If you say so." Violet was less than convinced, considering that Zandr had probably never experienced what she was. She wished it was all a dream, but she had no idea what she would awaken to. The mere concept was terrifying.

Realizing that they were wasting time, she started out ahead of him.

She had to concentrate on something else. Anything! She lifted her gaze then almost gasped as a thought struck her. This world was far too large for her. She imagined that it might be equivalent to seeing the Earth from outer space. The planet no longer seemed quite the same after viewing it from the stars' point of view. What was once thought of being so big was small in comparison and vice versa. It was difficult to walk through what seemed like a jungle, but at her normal size it would be more like a patch of weeds. She really wished there was a better way to travel. It was distressing to imagine how insignificant she was now.

What if someone stepped on her by accident? Her life would be over in a blink of an eye. It was a sad thought. She wondered if anyone else felt the same way. Maybe this was why all the fairies seemed so sad. They no longer felt like themselves and were in fact, at a huge disadvantage now. It was tragic in a way— much more so than she could ever imagine. The question that swam through her head was if she was even capable enough to break such a curse? Much of her life had been dictated… at least as far as the memories of having two parents went.

Yet, the fairies were counting on her. She didn't want to live her life as nothing more than a disappointment. If she could prove herself as able to achieve something on her own, that would mean the world to her.

"Are you all right?" Zandr inquired as he picked up his pace to match hers.

"I may not understand what is going on, but if there is a way to fix things, then I want to at least try. The sooner we reach the castle, the closer to the answers we may be."

"It's a slim chance."

"It's the best we have."

He nodded. "Then I shall continue to offer my aid in any form I can."

Violet smiled. She just hoped she wasn't kidding herself.

Chapter 27

Violet tried to stay as confident as possible, but deep down she was afraid that she lacked the courage to succeed. She didn't want to be a disappointment. At least, Zandr was willing to help her. Perhaps if they worked together they would be able to free the fairies from the curse. That thought, however, did not ease her nerves. Neither did the doubt that began creeping into her head.

After all, how could she find something that she didn't know for sure existed? It was disconcerting the more she thought about it. Such a question may or may not exist, let alone the answer. How would she know what it looked like or what it really was? It was irksome that she had some many questions that kept popping up, yet no answers. Was there no end to this endless river she was caught in?

Violet frowned as she considered the other questions. Where was the Crystal Garden? How could she get there? How could she break the curse? Where did she have to go to do so? Who was she really? Why was a field mouse wanting to marry her off to a mole? What was actually real? Was she really chosen to save this land? Who could she trust? Was she even capable of making a proper decision? The more she thought about the multiplying questions, the more stressed she became. Was there no end to them? She wasn't sure if she would ever find that answer. The only thing she knew, was to take the advice she had been given and follow her heart. Violet pondered how easy that would be. Could she avoid mishearing it so she wouldn't make a bad choice? She didn't want to fail. This was the first time that others believed in her. She couldn't fail them. Not now. Not ever. That was all there was to it. She didn't want to be a disappointment ever again. Not if she could help it.

It just wasn't fair. As hard as she tried, she just couldn't get anything right. It was pathetic. Nothing worked and all she did was make more problems. How could she even consider breaking a curse if she had no clue where to start?

"Are you all right?"

Her head snapped up at the sound of Zandr's voice. She blinked several times, as though coming out of a trance. "What?"

He frowned at her. "I said I miss the birds."

"Where did they go?"

"No one knows. They just disappeared and never returned." He smiled as though recalling a fond memory. "They were excellent companions. They always helped us whenever they could."

Violet found that a bit strange. She wondered if it could have had something to do with the curse. "Maybe you'll see them again someday."

"I hope so."

"How much further?"

Zandr glanced at her over his shoulder. "A few hours I think. Don't worry, we'll make it."

"Okay."

The breeze fluffed at his dark unruly hair. He narrowed his eyes as they navigated around a tree. "This was much easier human-sized."

"I wouldn't argue against that." She hesitated a moment before asking something that was on her mind. "Why are you not with your family? You look to be around my age-"

"Just drop it."

"But-"

"They have no need for me in the castle. They already have their successors to the throne. I'm not necessary." With that Zandr sped up his pace.

Violet fell silent for a moment. "I guess you come from a large family."

"I told you all this earlier and I don't wish to discuss it any further."

"I'm an only child."

"Good for you."

Violet shook her head. "I didn't mean it like that. If I had other siblings perhaps my parents wouldn't be so controlling over what I can and cannot do."

"That's a part of growing up in any family. There are always rules."

"Not like mine. My mother-" Violet cried out as a shock pain lanced through her skull. Her bow slipped out of her grasp as she dropped to her knees clutching at her head with her free hand. Flashes of images raced through her mind, making her feel nauseated. Faces clashed with others violently. Two in particular were of very different women. One had fiery red hair and a fierce bitterness in her eyes while the other was fair haired with a kind gaze. Violet had to fight the urge to vomit. "What is wrong with me? I feel like I'm going to be split in half!"

Zandr knelt in front of her, gripping her shoulders. "Calm down. You shall be all right. Just hold on."

Tears rushed from her closed eyes as she began to whimper. "It hurts…"

As Zandr moved towards Violet, they heard a dark chuckle. The pair lifted their gazes to discover the Woodlin Queen stood a mere few feet away. Things had just gone from bad to worse.

Chapter 28

"Leave us. We have nothing you want," Zandr growled, drawing a dagger as he stood in between Violet and their foe.

The Woodlin Queen, however, smirked as she twisted her whip in her clawed hands. "On the contrary, the girl is mine. Hand her over now, or else I will set my army upon your pathetic kingdom."

"You don't have enough men to achieve that threat."

"Little do you know, you foolish prince."

Violet clenched her teeth together as she struggled against the pain. She forced her shaky hands to notch an arrow to the string of her bow. "Why do you want me so bad?"

The queen laughed. "Poor child. Does your head ache? I can take all the pain away if you come with me."

"I would rather die."

"That could be arranged as well."

Zandr's eyes narrowed with rage as he charged at their adversary, dagger positioned to strike. He saw the Woodlin Queen move her whip too late to dodge. He gasped a strangling breath as the long braid of leather wrapped around his throat, choking him.

"Zandr!" Violet cried out in vain as the fairy prince's fell to his knees, straining to free himself. "Let him go!"

The Woodlin Queen yanked him forward, forcing him to collapse to his stomach. "He attacked me. Now if you don't wish to watch his life wither away, drop your weapons and come with me."

"What?"

There was something about the Woodlin Queen that put Violet's back up. She didn't think she could fight back. Her heart pounded in her chest as she stared into the menacing, dark eyes. Zandr was beginning to lose consciousness.

"I will not repeat myself, girl. Either you come with me or he dies."

Violet clenched her jaw. She couldn't let Zandr die. That guilt would consume her whole. Instead she dropped her head, allowing her bow to fall to the ground. "You win."

The queen laughed with glee as Violet walked towards her in surrender. She released the fairy prince. "Very good. I have someone very eager to see you again. Come along, child."

"Yes, ma'am." Violet removed her quiver then trailed off without a struggle. Her energy felt drained, yet she didn't understand why. At least her head wasn't killing her any longer. *Please stay safe, Zandr. I'm sorry I couldn't help you.*

Chapter 29

$\mathcal{V}$iolet groaned as she felt something cool pressed against her forehead. She winced as drops of water seeped in from the corners of her closed eyelids. "Stop…"

"There, there. You had quite the fever, dear. Just lay still and relax," a sickly-sweet voice purred in her ear.

With a gasp, Violet bolted upright then stared in horror at the field mouse. "You!"

"Yes, it's me, Thumbelina. Who else could I be?" The mouse giggled, "Now that you seem to be much better, we can continue work on your gown for the wedding!"

"But… I was captured by the Woodlins. How did I get here? Zandr-"

"There is no such thing. It was all a dream from when you fell ill. No worries. You don't seem to be in danger any longer."

Violet touched her face then felt her head swim. "This doesn't make sense! My name isn't Thumbelina… It's Violet… Why can't I remember the rest of my name?"

"Dreams fade. It's normal."

"No, this isn't right. I'm human… I have a mother…" Her eyes crossed as two women's faces appeared in her mind. One was a severe looking red head while the other had soft wheat blonde colored hair and kind brown eyes. Violet's head pounded as the images clashed as though they fought for dominance in her memories. She turned away from the mouse and vomited.

"Looks like you're still a bit ill. No, worries. We will fix you right up. Wait here and I'll go fetch some soup." The field mouse rushed off leaving Violet alone in the tiny room.

When she lifted her gaze she noted that she seemed to be underground once again. That meant the mouse was the same one that wanted to marry her off to the mole. Sick or not, she still refused to go through with the marriage.

"I need to get out of here," Violet gasped. With shaky hands she pushed herself up. Her lips curved in a frown at not seeing her shoes anywhere in sight. She noted that she had been changed into yet another dress. This one was also white but covered in lace with the same pink ribbon. She didn't care so much about the dress, but the shoes on the other hand... she didn't want to have to go barefoot again!

"Use the fury. It'll be a good thing. Now to find an exit," she told herself, feeling lucid enough to walk around.

Violet crept out of the room, which she decided was quite simple since it lacked a door. She hoped she didn't run into either the mouse or the mole. They would be tricky to fight off, especially since she still felt dizzy. She had to force her feet to move and resist the urge to throw up again.

Keep going. Don't stop, she coaxed herself, tip-toeing down the dark tunnel. She could feel herself tremble as cold sweat ran down her back. She wanted to collapse to her knees. She felt so sick. What was wrong with her? Tears of frustration flooded her eyes. She couldn't let herself stop. Not now.

To Violet's horror, her legs gave out. She wanted to cry, but instead bit her lip hard. If she had to make herself crawl out of the earth then so be it. She would return to the surface again!

Mustering all the strength she could, she forced her arms and legs to move. She couldn't give up now. She had a task to accomplish. Despite the fact that her mind was all muddled, it was the one thing that seemed to stand out the most in the tangled mess. The Crystal Garden.

She could hear movement in the distance. Violet scrambled into the next tunnel as fast as she could, praying that no one heard. She pressed her back to the wall terrified that someone would find her.

The world seemed to spin as she squeezed her eyes shut and held her breath. She dug her nails into the soil that made up the floor until she had two good handfuls.

"Thumbelina!

Violet waited until the mouse's footfalls were almost on top of her then jumped to her feet as she threw the dirt into the mouse's eyes. The rodent shrieked, rubbing at her face in pain. Violet scooped up two more handfuls and took off at a sprint down the hall.

As she rounded another corner, she came to a sudden halt at the sight of a sun ray. There was an opening nearby! She just had to find it before the field mouse caught up to her. She picked up her pace, running as fast as she could towards the light. She smiled at it grew brighter— she was almost home free. A few feet more and she could catch glimpses of the sky. The smile faded when she looked up and realized that the opening was too high up to climb.

Filled with despair she dropped to her knees. She was so close. Freedom was within reach, yet so far away. "Now what am I going to do?"

Chapter 30

*I*t wasn't fair! Violet had endured a lot in her life, and just when it seemed like she could turn things around, she instead got slapped in the face. She wanted to weep tears of frustration over her short lived victory. Now it seemed it was all for nothing. Even worse, she still felt quite ill.

She wished someone could help her change what seemed to be her inescapable fate. She was too powerless to stop it by herself.

Snap out of it! A pity party isn't going to get you anywhere. So use that brain of yours and find a way! Violet couldn't believe she had just stooped to lecturing herself, but at least the berating seemed to help her refocus.

She was thankful that the field mouse had, yet to track her down. She knew her time was short, but it was better than nothing. Feeling calmer, she rose to her feet then peered at the large hole. Perhaps if she had a rope she could hook it onto one of the jagged rocks poking out.

Her gaze fell to the pink sash. She smiled. Unweaving it from around her waist, she tied a loop at the end. It would be tricky, and she didn't even know if it would work, however that wouldn't stop her from giving it a shot.

It took a few tries, but Violet managed ensnared one of the rocks. She gave it a good tug, then drew a deep breath. She had never rock climbed before. This adventure might prove to be her undoing.

With a firm grip she pulled herself up. She tried to use her feet to find some sort of leverage. To her horror she was unable to fully lift her weight and fell back down.

Frustrated, Violet pounded a fist on the ground. If only she had more upper body strength. Her mind shifted back to the bow, which must have gotten left behind.

She was worthless. How could anyone expect her to accomplish anything let alone break a curse? It was no wonder she was so easily controlled; she couldn't do anything for herself. Maybe it was best to surrender as she had countless times. "It's useless. I'm never going to amount to anything."

Her mind flitted to the image of the gentle blonde haired woman for a second. Shame washed over her. Why did she feel so guilty all of a sudden? It didn't make sense.

Was this even her world? She couldn't seem to remember how she got there to begin with. Was she looking for something? What was she supposed to do? Her head started to pound. With how much pain she felt, it was evident that this was not a dream. She just wished she could piece together the fragments that were her mind. It was disconcerting how much seemed to fade the more time passed by. One thing was for sure, she had to get out of there. She wasn't sure what she was running from, but her gut instincts screamed that she was in danger. Until she could figure out what was going on, the best thing she could do was trust herself.

She turned back to the wall nearest the opening and started digging with her hands. She hoped if she was lucky she could create a slope then use that to crawl out. A voice in the back of her head whispered disapproval in her digging in the dirt. Violet didn't care how filthy she got. As long as she found a way out that was all that mattered. Dirt was caked under her nails and her dress was no longer white, yet she didn't care. She'd crawl through the mud if it meant she would be free.

Soil tumbled down upon her from above. She gritted her teeth and scooped up even more. She would succeed. She had to.

Her arms burned with an aching pain, but she continued to push herself. She wouldn't let herself stop until she was back in the warm sunlight.

Just as she seemed to near her goal, a loud rumbling unsettled what she thought had been a sturdy slope, forcing her back into the tunnels.

"No!" Violet clawed at the dirt in despair. Why did her every attempt have to end in failure? She didn't want to be controlled anymore. It was her life. She would find a way to live it the way she wanted to if it was the last thing she did!

A burst of light flashed in front of her revealing a long stemmed crystal rose the color of rose quartz. She stared at it in wonder, pondering what it could mean. She reached a hesitant hand toward it then touched it. The flower disappeared as a rush, unlike she had felt before, filled her.

Violet glanced down in amazement at the sight of the pink dress with short sleeves cut to resemble flower petals. The knee length skirt shared the same motif. Jeweled butterflies accented the bodice, drifting down to the skirt. Around her waist were several interwoven ribbons, the ends flowed behind her like a small train. On her feet were silver sandals which wrapped around her legs up to her knees. It was a very simple, yet elegant look.

She returned her attention back to the hole then closed her eyes. A feeling of floating swirled around her. When Violet reopened her eyes, she gasped in shock at the iridescent wings that seemed to miraculously support her weight. "I can fly?"

A surge of energy exploded in her as she flew faster out of the darkness, reuniting with the light once again. Laughter bubbled out of her at the sight of the glorious sun. She had done it. She was free! Her memories were still shredded, but at least she was no longer trapped. Now all she needed to do was figure out what she had to do next.

Chapter 31

After flying for several minutes Violet was still at a loss. She was growing more frustrated as she struggled to recall whatever pieces of her memory she could. Drowning in despair, she landed on a tree branch. If only there was someone that could give her a hint. Just a tiny one was all she needed.

"Thumbelina? What are you doing here? Where is the prince?" A red haired fairy boy inquired from the branch above her.

She gasped, backing away. "Who are you? And what are you talking about? What prince?"

"You don't remember me?" The boy asked, confused. When she shook her head he sighed in disappointment. "I'm Ash. My father gave you some shoes earlier."

"I'm sorry. Nothing is familiar."

He pouted at her answer. "Wait right there. I'm going to get my mother. Stay put!"

Before she could ask another question he zoomed off.

Violet twisted her fingers with her hands. She wished she had some sort of clue as to what was going on. Everything was unnerving. She hated feeling so lost. Sure she had achieved a great gift in being able to fly, but something still felt very wrong deep down inside of her. She couldn't remember who she was or what she was going to do. Everything was a horrible blank that made her want to scream in frustration.

"Oh you poor thing," a brunette woman cooed as she landed front from of the confused strawberry blonde.

Violet backed away in fear. "Please don't hurt me."

"Ash was right," the female fairy whispered. She reached a gentle hand out to the frightened girl. "It's okay, I won't hurt you. I promise. The little boy you met a moment ago is my son. I gave you and the prince food earlier."

Violet shook her head. "I don't remember. Can you help me? I want my memories back."

"What can you recall?"

"Nothing. It's all hazy and broken." Violet dropped to her knees hugging herself. "I don't understand what is going on. Why is this happening to me?"

"Calm down." The woman knelt in front of her, placing her hands on Violet's shoulders. "We'll take care of you. I promise."

Violet trembled as tears flooded her eyes. A piercing shock of pain stabbed into her skull. She cried out in agony, almost falling off the branch but was pulled away from the edge just in time by the woman.

The boy flew towards his mother in concern. "Mama?"

"Bring Garis here immediately!" She shouted to Ash as she cradled Violet close to her. Once the boy obeyed she returned her attention back to the girl. "It's okay. Just relax. We'll get you healed. Stay calm. Hang in there."

Violet whimpered, burying her face in the woman's shoulder. "Please… I don't want to die."

She could hear a muffled sound before all went black.

Chapter 32

Violet blinked confusion at finding herself in a room clouded in white. She picked herself off the floor then almost jumped at the sight of a blonde girl clothed in a lavender gown. "Who… are you?"

The girl scowled at the question. "Odd. Upon receiving your rose you should have remembered who you are. You shouldn't be in this state…"

Tears fell from Violet's amber eyes. "Please, tell me who I really am. Everything is so confusing. I feel like I'm going to go insane trying to make sense of all this!"

"I'm afraid even if I do, it will get lost. You must defeat the one that has cursed you before you lose your memories completely. You must be cautious. I am sorry for not being able to do more for you."

"I'm cursed?" The word caught in her throat. "Who did this to me?"

"You wouldn't remember even if I told you." The girl gave her a sad smile. "Nonetheless, my name is Lunette. We have met before."

"We have?" Violet lowered her gaze then widened it at the sight of the unfamiliar pink dress. "Why am I wearing this?"

Lunette shook her head. "I wish I could do more for you. It shouldn't have happened this way."

"What is wrong with me?"

"The curse has fragmented your mind. Truth and fiction has splintered causing massive confusion. It's like your mind is a mirror and it has been smashed to the point that you can barely see yourself through the cracks."

Violet frowned. "I still don't understand…"

Lunette pressed her hand to the strawberry blonde haired girl's forehead. "Seek out Zandr. He will help you. Don't give up until you find him."

"Will I be able to remember this?"

"I'm not certain." The blonde's violet gaze was melancholy with a tinge of concern. "Please be extra cautious. There is no telling what your enemy has in store for you next."

Violet took a soothing breath. For some reason the strange girl seemed to have a calming effect on her. "I will try."

Lunette took Violet's hands in hers. "Be safe. You are more important than you may perceive yourself to be."

With that said everything around Violet faded away.

Chapter 33

Violet bolted upright to find herself on the small table in what appeared to be a room inside a tree. She frowned in confusion. This didn't look familiar either. Then she realized that she wasn't alone.

Several people she didn't recognize stared at her in bewilderment. Fearful, she scrambled down to the floor in a desperate attempt to get as far away from them as possible.

The elder man snatched her hand before she could run. "Easy there."

She jerked back, her heart thudded in her chest as she looked back at the group of strangers. "Who are you? Where am I? Why am I here?"

He didn't reply. Instead he shook his head, addressing the group. "This is rather alarming. She really has seemed to have lost her memory."

The woman bent over Violet, her face washed with concern. "Can you recall anything, dear?"

Violet narrowed her eyes, struggling to bring anything into focus. What she got instead was a sharp pain to her head. She cried out as it shot through her skull. "No!"

The white haired man sighed, "I don't like this. I think something was done to her, but I can't put my finger on what."

"What are we going to do? She can't survive like this!" the brunette woman glanced at the girl, worry shining in her gaze.

"I'm afraid that any healing spells I use might make matters worse."

"We have to do something."

Violet shook her head as she backed away. Staying there was pointless, especially since she didn't know who they were or if they could be trusted. "Please, don't fight. It's my body, I will just have to live with whatever is wrong with me."

"But-"

"Thank you for your hospitality. I must go." Before anyone could argue she raced off, taking to the skies once she was back outside. For some reason the only thing that seemed to echo in her head was a single name. Zandr. She had to find him. Somehow.

Chapter 34

*W*hy was this happening to her? Why couldn't she remember anything? Violet's distress increased as she found herself forced to land. She had spent all of her wings' energy without realizing it. What good was it to be able to fly when you couldn't go long distances? It seemed quite ludicrous. She just wanted to go home… wherever that was.

Amber eyes glanced around the unfamiliar forest. To say she was afraid was a severe understatement. She didn't have the slightest clue of what to do or where to go. It was so frustrating!

Tears blurred her vision as she tried to come up with some sort of a plan, but she had no idea where she was or where she needed to go. She was stuck.

Breathe. You'll figure this out. Just calm down. She hoped she had travelled far enough away from the mouse. The last thing she wanted was to find herself trapped underground once again.

The tall stalks of grass towered above her as she wandered through the thick foliage. She pushed them out of the way with her hands, enabling her the ability to move easier.

"What am I doing? This is pointless!" She said aloud, stomping her foot in aggravation. She shouldn't have left the fairies. They could have provided her with some useful information. Now she had no way of knowing if she was even going the right way.

Zandr, where are you? Who are you for that matter? Why am I even looking for you to begin with?

Annoyed with herself, Violet plopped down on a rock. She felt so pathetic. If only she had stopped to come up with some sort of a plan, rather than fly off without thinking, she wouldn't be in this mess! She buried her face in her hands wishing for an answer to her problem.

"Excuse me?"

Her head snapped up at the sound of a deep male voice. She whirled around to find what she guessed was a male fairy with long dark hair and intense gray eyes. "Are you Zandr?"

"Zandr?" He blinked in puzzlement then grinned. "You must be speaking of my younger brother."

Violet scrambled off her rock, relieved to be speaking to someone who knew who she was seeking out. "Do you know where I can find him?"

"Sure. I can take you to him."

"Wonderful!" She was delighted to no longer be alone. It appeared that her luck was at last turning around. "My name is Violet. What is yours?"

"Osric."

"It's nice to meet you."

He nodded, then held out his hand. "Shall we?"

Violet hesitated a moment before accepting. He was Zandr's brother after all… or so he said. Still, he was the best chance she had to make any progress.

"Okay."

Chapter 35

Violet allowed Osric to lead her by the hand through the vast forest. A part of her longed to ask question after question yet another... wasn't so sure if she should. Maybe it was the amnesia that was making her feel less talkative. After all, she had no real experiences to share. All she had was her name.

"So, how much further?" she inquired.

"Not too far," the man replied, shoving aside a few leaves.

"You can let go of me. I should be okay."

He gave her a kind smile. "Nonsense. I just want to keep you safe."

Violet bit her lip unsure of how to respond to that. She felt very awkward and hoped it didn't show. Brushing her bangs from her eyes she nodded. "Well then, thank you."

"Don't mention it."

Her eyes narrowed as an odd feeling stirred in her belly. Osric seemed to be a nice person, however his words didn't match the tone in his voice. There was something off that the longer she was with him, the more uncertain she felt. She was beginning to wish she hadn't accepted his hand.

Violet drew a deep breath, "Listen, not to be rude, but I'd like you to let go now."

Osric stopped dead. Without warning he whirled on her, his grip tightening enough to bruise. "Not until we have reached our destination."

"You're hurting me!" She cried out as fear burst to life, numbing the pain his hold on her had caused.

The fairy sneered. "That's nothing. You're mine now."

Violet's eyes widened in horror when she was yanked towards him then lifted into his arms as wings formed on his back. She tried to squirm her way out of his clutches, but he wouldn't release her. "Put me down! I need to see Zandr!"

He chuckled, lifting off the ground, taking flight. "You won't see that disgrace ever again."

"Let go!" On the last word, as her fist beat down on his back, a rush of wind tore her from his arms. She screamed as she tumbled in the air, falling fast towards the hard earth. She pressed her hands down, bracing herself for impact then gasped in shock as a cushion of air formed under her. "What did I just do?"

"Get back here," Osric dove at her, his arms outstretched to snatch her from where she floated.

Violet lifted her hands blasting him backwards with a gust of wind. She squeezed her eyes shut, begging for her wings to reappear. With a flash of light, her wish had been granted. She took off to the sky as fast as she could, with a single goal in mind—to get as far away from Osric as possible.

Chapter 36

Hot tears fell from Violet's amber eyes as she dropped to the ground, shaking and out of breath. She didn't know where she was or who she could trust for that matter. She was alone, completely scared out of her mind. Why did she have to be so stupid by leaving the other fairies? Now she was in very real danger. She didn't know what Osric's intentions were, but she doubted she would like them. He might not even be Zandr's brother.

At least she had a way to defend herself. She possessed the power of air. She didn't understand why she had it, but it was better than nothing.

Violet sat on the ground, pulling her knees to her chest as she buried her face in them. Why did she have to get amnesia now? She hated feeling like a big blank. It frightened her. Why did all her memories disappear? Was there a way to get them back?

Zandr.

Her gut told her to find him, although she still had yet to come up with the reason why. It didn't make sense. How did she even know that finding this… person wouldn't put her in danger? It could be a trap for all she knew.

You can't just sit here forever. She groaned, knowing her thoughts were correct. She had to come up with some sort of a solution to her predicament.

The question was what? After a long silent debate she decided that her best answer was to find some people and ask them if they knew anything about Zandr. In order to do that, however, she would need to pick a direction and start walking. It was a gamble, but she had few other choices.

Rising to her feet Violet closed her eyes as she spun around with one arm outstretched, pointing in front of her. Her only thought was to find Zandr, as she came to a halt.

"Please let this be the right way to him," she whispered, walking in the direction she had pointed to.

To Violet's surprise, it didn't take too long before she found herself facing a stream. Relieved to find something other than grass, she sprinted towards it. Kneeling down, she scooped some water into her cupped hand then took a sip. It felt so good going down her parched throat that she sighed in pleasure. She drank until she had her fill then headed upstream. She hoped she was going in the right direction. Only time would tell.

Chapter 37

Violet sighed as she continued to follow the stream. So far her journey had been rather uneventful. She supposed that was for the best. She was glad that there were no signs of any potential threats. She didn't think she could take much more excitement.

She still felt uneasy at having no memories. How would she know who she could trust? Someone could pretend to be Zandr and she wouldn't know any better. It was unnerving.

I'm not going to worry about that now. I just need to stick to the plan. I'll figure out where to go from there. She drew back her shoulders in determination. She wouldn't allow herself to give in to the fear filled voice whispering in the back of her head.

With that thought in mind, she shoved at a mass of thick grass. She was growing tiresome of walking, but wasn't sure if she had allowed… whatever it was that gave her the ability to fly— to regain the energy it had used up. The idea that she had the power over air confused her a great deal. Did she always have the ability? Or did it come with the new clothing she was wearing?

Violet frowned down at her pink dress. There was so much of herself and the world that she didn't know.

She hoped to find the answers soon. Until then she would have to keep going until she found the truth.

Her thoughts shattered as the ground pulsed beneath her. The thunderous quaking became more violent with each passing minute until she could no longer keep her balance. Violet squeezed her eyes shut trying to make her wings appear. She breathed a sigh of relief when the bright light flashed around her. Quick as lightning, she took off to the sky and almost collided into a giant with long golden blonde hair riding a horse.

She screamed in horror, as a large hand swatted at her. In defense she hit him with a burst of wind then narrowly avoid being hit again in retaliation.

"Alphonse, stop! Don't hurt her," a feminine voice shouted in warning from behind.

Violet spun around, but it was too late. A second pair of hands closed in around her.

"Calm, down. I'm not going to harm you," the female soothed as she cradled the small girl in her hands.

Amber eyes met icy blue as Violet stood in the gentle hand. A strange feeling of déjà vu rushed through her as she stared at the dark haired girl with pale skin. "Who are you?"

"My name is Bianca, but I'm also known as Snow White. I'm guessing that you must be Thumbelina."

"You're mistaken. My name is Violet."

Bianca smiled. "Another of your names. You and I are special. I have the power over ice and you over air. There is also a quest which must be completed."

"How do you know this?"

"Because I'm like you."

Violet frowned as confusion washed over her. "You're a lot bigger than me."

"That's because I am human-sized while you are fairy-sized." Bianca laughed with amusement.

"Then who is he?" the small girl pointed to the young man near them. "He tried to hit me."

"That's Alphonse, my fiancé. He's safe. You just took him by surprise."

"I apologize for that." The young man scratched the back of his head in embarrassment. "You are the first fairy I have ever come across."

Violet nodded. She was still amazed that there were giants around. It must have been a miracle that she had never been stepped on. "I guess no hard feelings then."

"Is there someplace you're trying to go?" Bianca inquired, drawing Violet's attention back to her. "If it's along our way, we could take you there."

"I don't know where I am going to be honest."

"What do you mean?"

"I don't remember much of anything," Violet sighed as she shoved her curls from her face. "All I do know is that I need to find Zandr, but I have no idea who or where he is. It's horribly frustrating."

Bianca exchanged concerned glances with Alphonse. "You've received your flower though. That doesn't seem possible."

"Well, it is." Violet then shared everything she could remember up to the moment she encountered Alphonse. "I'm starting to get hungry too."

"That I can fix." The princess turned to her fiancé. "Can you tear off a tiny portion of bread?"

He nodded and did as she asked before passing it to her.

Bianca gave it to Violet who wolfed it down. "Better?"

"Much."

"I'd rather not leave you on your own especially with that mouse and Osric looking for you."

"I appreciate it." Violet kept her balance Bianca moved her to the horse's head. She smiled at how soft the snowy white mane was. "I think if you can get me as close to the waterfall as possible, I might be okay."

"Very well." Bianca gave her horse a whistle then started off at a walk with Alphonse and his stallion close behind.

Chapter 38

It was nice being able to travel a larger distance in a shorter time span, Violet decided. Being able to talk to Bianca somehow made her feel a small amount of relief. She felt like she could trust her for some reason. She and even Alphonse, despite their previous encounter, made Violet feel safe. She had fun listening to Bianca's stories of her travels and how she came to be the person she was today.

The thing that intrigued Violet the most was the mentioning of the quest. Something about that word was familiar. Had she met someone like Bianca before, but forgot about the encounter?

"Are there any others like you?" Violet flinched, realizing she had spoken her question aloud.

"Like me?" The raven haired girl pursed her lips then nodded. "Did she have long brown hair and green eyes?"

The face flashed through Violet's mind so fast she almost slipped off the mare's head. "Yes!"

"That would have been Cybele or Rapunzel as she is known in her land."

"How many of us are there?"

"Currently? Three, but by the year's end, six."

Alphonse scowled. "Don't you think you are telling her too much?"

"She needs more information than Cybele did," Bianca explained. "I'm not certain what happened to your memories. Perhaps you'll regain them once you finish the quest."

Violet scrunched her nose in confusion. "But you said I already have received my Crystal Rose."

"That's the first step, however, you have more to go. For each person, the quest is different."

"So, you can't tell me what I have to do."

"I'm afraid not."

Violet sighed as she gave Bianca a sad smile. "It's all right. You've helped me more than anyone else has. I appreciate it."

"All I ask of you is to complete your quest and seek out Lunette. She will need all the help she can get when her time comes," the raven haired princess murmured. "Her curse will be much more difficult to break than any of the others."

"Why?"

"I cannot say. I only request your aid in exchange for ours."

Violet narrowed her eyes then nodded. "I am not certain what help I will be, but I shall do my best."

To her relief the ride continued without incident. Violet guessed that being on top of a massive animal with two giant companions had its advantages. She was almost disappointed when they reached her destination. She sighed as she took in the large majestic waterfall then lowered her gaze to its torrential stream.

"I'm sorry we can't take you any closer," Bianca said as she climbed down from her mount. She held out her palm to Violet, allowing the girl to steady herself before moving towards a stone.

"You have done more than enough. It would take me forever to walk this far on my own. Thank you," she smiled up at the princess before hoping off the girl's hand.

"Good luck on your quest."

Violet bid Bianca a safe journey before watching the princess and prince ride off. She turned to the stream then lifted her gaze to the waterfall. Something about it registered in her mind, but she was unable to remember due to all the fog. Still… what did she have to lose?

With that thought in mind, she headed towards the cliff, hoping to find a pathway up.

Chapter 39

"*N*ow how do I get up there? Is it worth even flying?" Violet muttered to herself, evaluating the height of the cliff face. She didn't want to underestimate the distance then find herself crashing into the water below. She might not survive the fall.

She rubbed at her face, pushing her bangs from her eyes. She couldn't give up. Not now. There had to be some way up. Her thoughts were interrupted at the sound of someone calling out to her. She whirled around in fright to find a dark haired male fairy flying towards her.

"It really is you! How did you escape the Woodlin Queen?"

Violet drew back in fear. "Stay away from me."

Silver eyes narrowed in confusion at her words. "Do you not remember me? It's Zandr."

Her heart skipped a beat in hope, but she clenched the emotion tight. "Prove it."

"What do you mean? We met hours ago. You were kidnapped… What did the queen do to you?" He looked her over, taking in her appearance. "You've changed clothes."

Violet bit her lip. "Unless you can prove to me that you are who you say you are, then leave me be. I refused to be fooled again."

"Again?" He shoved a hand through his messy hair in frustration. "Look, my kingdom is just above our heads. If you let me take you there then the Fairy King and Queen will vouch for me. Otherwise we're at a stalemate. I promise to not do you any harm. You have my word."

"How do I know that this is not a trick?"

Zandr sighed. "You don't. You just need to trust me."

Violet refused to drop her guard despite wanting to believe he was telling her the truth. "The last time I trusted someone, they said they were your brother then tried to kidnap me."

The fairy prince took a step towards her, and came to a halt as she began to back away. He held up his hands to prove he was nonthreatening. "Who?"

Tears stung Violet's eyes as the memory resurfaced. "He said his name was Osric. I had to fight him off."

"That makes no sense…" He shook his head. "No matter. Let me take you to my parents. They might know who we can ask for more information on your quest."

Her eyes widened. "You know about my quest?"

"We discussed it earlier." He frowned, tilting his head in thought. "Perhaps you should see the royal healer as well. Did you hit your head?"

A blush tinted her cheeks. "I don't remember. I don't think so."

He moved to grab her, but she shoved him away.

"What are you doing?" Her voice trembled with panic.

"I was going to carry you. How else are you going to get up there?"

Violet debated on whether or not to try flying up herself before she closed her eyes, wishing for her wings to return.

Zandr gasped in shock. "You have wings... You really are Thumbelina."

"Do you promise to help me if I can't make it all the way up on my own? I can't seem to travel long distances."

"You have my word." He held out a hand to her as his own silvery wings appears. Violet hesitated before accepting. She drew a deep breath before they took to the sky together.

Chapter 40

Violet was taken aback by the size of the fairy castle. It looked as though it were built for Bianca and Alphonse sized people. It was at least three stories tall, with a flower garden, two towers at opposite sides, stained glass windows, and a large draw bridge.

It also seemed eerily empty, but Violet guessed that was because the inhabitants were all very small like she was. "You live here? It's enormous!"

"Not really when you consider how many people live on the grounds. However, with the curse in place that prevents us from changing our size, yes, it is way too big now." He stepped forward and nodded at one of the guards stationed at the door. "Glendl"

The guard saluted him as he stepped aside. "Prince Zandr…"

The fairy prince took Violet's hand, pulling her through the threshold with him. "It has been a while since I was last here. It's good to see that nothing has changed in my absence."

Violet goggled at the large tapestries, suits of armor, and shields decorating the walls. Everything was so breathtaking. "This is incredible!"

"It's even better when we are bigger. The castle is usually decorated to suit whatever occasion. It's a little hard to do so now with being stuck as small as we are."

"Even so, it's the most beautiful place I have ever seen!" She gasped in awe. "I could never imagine living here though. I would be afraid of being scolded for doing something wrong."

"My family isn't that strict. They have their rules, but leave room for us to make and learn by our mistakes."

"That is very fortunate."

For whatever reason Violet was quite nervous to meet Zandr's family. What would they be like? Would they even like her? Just thinking about it was stressing her out. She didn't want to be met with disapproval.

He came to a halt then glanced back at her. "Are you all right?"

"Fine. Why?"

"You fell silent. Relax, it's going to be okay."

"If you say so." She bit her lip, unsure of why she was feeling so comfortable with him. Perhaps it was because he had kept his promise and never tried to hurt her. Still, she couldn't let her guard down, not completely. After all, there was a chance that he wasn't Zandr after all. The simple thought was rather unsettling.

"Trust me," he said, leading her down the hall.

Violet said nothing as she trailed after him. It wasn't too much longer before they entered a lavish throne room. They had to fly to avoid being smothered by the plush runner.

"Zandr! What brings you here, young man?" A male fairy with graying dark hair and golden eyes flew towards his son. A woman with auburn hair and copper colored eyes joined him. "We weren't expecting you."

"Who is this?" The woman inquired, studying Violet with interest.

"Father, Mother, I would like you to meet Thumbelina-" the prince began.

"Violet, Your Majesties," she corrected. "My name is Violet."

The Fairy Queen smiled as she took Violet's hands. "Then the prophecy is true. You are the one who shall break us free from our curse."

"Do you know of anyone who can tell me more about my quest?"

"The healer should have some information that you might find useful."

Violet nodded. "Thank you. Where might I find him?"

"Zandr knows the way," the king said, gesturing to his son.

"Right," the prince shifted, then offered Violet his arm. "I can escort you to him. It's not too far."

The Queen patted Violet's hand. "No worries. We will have another conversation after you have seen the healer."

"All right." She accepted Zandr's arm as he guided her from the throne room. She was unsure what to think of everything, but at least for the moment, she was safe. There was no telling how long that would remain true.

Chapter 41

*I*t took little time before they reached what resembled a large library. Books as tall as buildings towered above from even larger bookcases. A white haired man pored over a particularly thick tome as his assistants stood at the edges of the pages awaiting orders.

Candles of various sizes, flickering with light, cast dancing shadows along the walls. Just like every room Violet had been in or had passed, it too was well furnished and decorated.

The old man lifted his head at the presence of the two newcomers. His crystal blue eyes sparkled at the sight of the prince. "Zandr! How good of you to visit me. And who is your lovely companion? Wait. Do not tell me. Are you the fair Thumbelina, my lady?"

Violet's jaw dropped as she was about to deny it, but something about the man's all-knowing tone made her reconsider whether or not she knew who she really was. After all, her memories were gone, so who was to say that they were not correct. "I... don't know. A part of me wants to say no, yet another is unsure of what to believe."

The fairy prince blinked in surprise at her answer. "She needs information regarding the Quest of the Crystal Garden. We were hoping you could be of some assistance."

The healer smiled as he approached the girl then took her hands in his. He closed his eyes and frowned. "You have been cursed, though I'm unsure what kind it is. Has anything peculiar occurred?"

"She cannot remember anything past maybe an hour ago." Zandr filled the healer in on everything that had happened up until the moment they had reached the castle. "Can you help her?"

The man released Violet. "I am afraid the magic is beyond anything I have ever seen. I am very sorry."

Violet sighed despite knowing that it was futile to hope for some sort of cure. It didn't make the disappointment she felt lessen. At least she wouldn't have to fear being steered in the wrong direction. "What about the quest? Can you tell me anything of the Crystal Garden or where I can find it?"

The healer gave her a sad smile. "All I know is that it is a special destiny, which you must fulfill in order to break the curse. Everything else you must find out on your own."

Another dead end. She was growing tiresome of running in circles. It seemed like whenever she found a possible solution to a problem she was proven wrong and instead found herself right back where she started. She wanted to grip at her hair as she screamed in frustration. Despite the strangling urge, she tightened her grip on self-control. She refused to have a temper tantrum in front of strangers.

Violet drew a soothing breath, fighting to keep herself calm. "Is there anything useful you can tell me? I feel like I am wandering around blind. If you wish me to break this curse I need some sort of a lead. Otherwise, I fear I won't be of any help."

The man studied her a moment before nodding. "You need to find the Sky Fortress."

"Do you know where it is? Can you provide a map?"

"I am afraid not. It is never in the same place for long, yet stays within the kingdom."

Violet tugged at one of her curls. "At least I won't have to run all over the world to find it. I guess that's a bit of a blessing."

Zandr took a step forward. "How can we locate the fortress?"

"You will have to find the fire cloud, though it is usually hidden in a blanket of other clouds," the healer explain.

"What is a fire cloud?" The prince scowled. "I have never heard of such a thing."

"It is what it sounds like, but is far more difficult to see than you may think. There have been very few sightings in the past several years."

"I see."

"I apologize for not being of more help, my lady," the man bowed with regret.

Violet bit her lip in thought. "No, it's all right. Do you know of anyone else that might be able to help?"

He shook his head. "I wish I could provide you with better news."

"Thank you for giving me what you could. I will do my best in ending the curse. I think, it may be the only solution to my problem at this point."

"I wish you all the luck in the world. Safe travels to you both." He slipped Zandr a small bag. "In case you need it."

"Thank you," the prince said, taken aback by the offering. "How did you know I would be going with her?"

The healer smiled. "I know far more than you can imagine, I just do not possess all the pieces of the great puzzle all at once."

"Well, then thank you," Zandr nodded a bit awkward as though befuddled by the man's statement. "We shall heed your words."

"Yes, thank you." Violet gave him a smile before Zandr escorted her out of the room.

"Did any of what he said make sense to you?" The prince whispered as they rushed off.

"Not a single word."

"Good, we shall bid my parents farewell then continue this quest of yours."

Violet frowned at him. "Why do you want to help me?"

"I already told you, I always keep my promises. Plus, you are our only hope."

Violet nodded. She hated having so much pressure on her shoulders, but that this point, she had no choice except to go through with the plan to save the kingdom. There were no other options left if she wanted her memories back. She just wished she knew for sure that breaking the curse meant she would be free from hers as well.

Chapter 42

*V*iolet glanced at Zandr as they walked through the grass towards the mountain behind the castle. She was grateful his parents had provided them with supplies including food for the journey. She was even given a bow and a quiver full of arrows, although she didn't understand why. Did she even know archery? Lacking memories had to be the most troublesome thing in the world!

One thing that confused her was that Zandr did not mention what she had told him about her encounter with his brother. When she inquired he shrugged.

"We do not know for certain that it was Osric that you spoke to. It could have very well been an imposter posing as him. After all, you two have never met," the fairy prince stated.

"True, but what if it was him? Why would he try to kidnap me?" She scrunched up her nose in thought. "You said that a Woodlin Queen had abducted me earlier, right?"

"Yes, that was the last time I saw you before the waterfall."

She pushed a curly strand of hair from her face. "I wish I could remember what happened to me after that point."

"That makes two of us."

Violet narrowed her eyes at him, but he looked away. Rather than press him for an explanation, she changed the subject. "So, are we wandering aimlessly or do we have a destination?"

"I know of another person we could consult. However, it won't be easy to reach her."

"Of course."

"What is that supposed to mean?"

She shrugged. "Just that nothing is simple around here."

He shook his head with a snort. "I can't say I could call you a liar."

Violet sighed. She was growing tired of traveling from place to place only to have less information than she started with. Everything was so confusing that she wasn't sure if it was even worth asking questions anymore.

They continued walking in silence until Zandr grabbed her wrist. When she looked at him in shock, he pointed up. "This is why I said we needed to walk a ways."

Violet's stomach lurched at the height. It was even worse than flying from the ground to the top of the waterfall. "I don't know if I'll be able to make it."

"You won't know unless you try."

She clenched her jaw. He had a point, however it didn't ease her unsettled stomached. Flying was still a new thing that she had yet to master. "If we have no other choice…"

"We don't." When she still seemed hesitant, Zandr added, "If you start wavering, I'll help you up the rest of the way."

Violet blew out a breath before nodding. "Okay. As long as you don't let me crash to the earth below, then I guess it won't hurt to try."

"Good-"

Zandr never finished his sentence as a burst of noxious gas swarmed them. Violet lost sight of him before she passed out.

Chapter 43

"You shouldn't be here."

Violet's eyelashes fluttered a moment before she managed to bring everything into focus. She was in a strange room with walls that resembled carved crystal. In the center were six pedestals. Three had clear roses floating above them, while three others glowed white, green, and pink.

"Where am I?"

"A place you shouldn't be," replied the feminine voice she heard earlier.

Standing before Violet, was a young woman with straight blonde hair pulled back into an elegant bun. She wore a pale pink dress trimmed in white feathers with a single white feather pinned to her hair.

"You don't need to be so rude. Who are you anyway?" The petite strawberry blonde inquired.

"My name is Grace, not that you will remember."

"And just what is that supposed to mean?"

Grace sniffed as she rolled her eyes. "Were you not listening? You should not be here! You have messed everything up."

Violet frowned, "What are you talking about? I don't even know where I am or how I got here."

The woman threw her hands in the air as she began to pace. "What does it matter? You have already doomed us all!"

"Will you stop being so melodramatic and tell me what is going on?"

Grace turned on her heel then scoffed. "Why should I explain anything to you? You have destroyed everything. We were so close, yet you had to fail!"

Violet was growing more agitated as the woman refused to answer her questions. "How can I even attempt to fix things, if you do not tell me what I did wrong?"

The woman lifted her hazel gaze to meet the teenaged girl's. Eyes that once held disdain for the petite strawberry blonde, filled with sorrow. "The curse. Something went wrong. You shouldn't be in such a state."

"You mean my lack of memories."

Grace nodded. "You should have remembered at least something of who you are, but you're blank It's a wonder that the Air Rose even came to you."

"So, the flower was real after all," Violet murmured in remembrance of the strange phenomenon that granted her the pink dress and the ability to use air magic.

"Yes, however, you haven't awoken its full potential. You haven't even grasped who you are."

Violet winced. "Then can you tell me? I want to make things right."

Grace shook her head. "I fear not. I can only provide you with a limited amount of knowledge, which you may or may not even remember."

"It's not like I wished for this to happen! I would very much like to have my memories back."

"Are you willing to face whatever challenges lay before you to complete your quest and break the curse?"

Violet closed her eyes a moment as she thought of those who had helped her. If they were counting on her then it would be selfish to turn her back on them. "Yes. Even if it means that I will remain an amnesiac for the rest of my life."

A delicate smile curved on Grace's lips. "Then perhaps hope is still alive after all. Keep that promise in your heart and never surrender."

Before Violet could ask anything more, her vision filled with white, blinding her of the crystal room. The Crystal Garden she realized, before all thoughts left her.

Chapter 44

A groan escaped Violet's lips as she tried to sit up. She blinked in confusion at finding herself sprawled out on what resembled a lily pad. Her heart lurched in her chest as a sensation of something being very wrong stirred in her belly.

She pushed her hair from her face, then scowled. It was damp. Now it was going to frizz! Could things get any worse?

A croaking sound made her scramble to her feet. Her eyes widened in horror at seeing a group of toads. "Oh no."

Violet glanced down at herself. Good, she was still wearing her pink dress. For some strange reason, she dreaded the thought of wearing white even though she couldn't figure out why. The word that seemed to echo in her head was, *run.*

She winced, her head was starting to pound. Her body wavered, fighting to maintain her balance. She had to get away somehow. Then she remembered— Zandr. Where was he?

All she could see around her was water and toads. Violet chewed on her lip, debating on what to do. She drew a breath and gave the amphibians a smile. "Thank you, but I really must be going. I have a friend that I must find. You don't by any chance know where he might be?"

Her only reply was croaking.

Violet rubbed her face in frustration. At least she should still have her powers. That meant she could fly away. However, just as she was about to call out her wings, a voice made her stop cold.

"Oh, yes! He's in the caves." A smaller toad pushed past the others. Something about it made Violet's skin crawl.

"Thank you. Then I shall-"

"You're not going anywhere, my dear."

Violet stared at the female toad in horror. It talked. Didn't she remember something about animals shouldn't be able to talk? Then why could this one? Perhaps she could hear and understand animal speech? Maybe it was another one of her abilities? However, something about it didn't sit right with her. If she could hear animal speech, then why couldn't she understand the other toads? It didn't make sense. There was something very strange going on.

Just as she turned to fly away, another face she didn't anticipate seeing appeared.

The fairy who called himself Osric, Zandr's older brother.

Chapter 45

How could things have gone from bad to worse in such a short period of time? Now if she took to the skies, she might be caught by the fairy that had attempted to trick her last time she had encountered him. Whether he really was Osric was another question. All she knew was that she wanted to get as far away from the lily pad as soon as possible.

Violet moved towards the edge of the large leaf, furthest away from both of her threats. If she had enough space between them, then perhaps she could escape before either had a chance to snatch her midair. Her gaze drifted to the water and she gulped. She didn't know how to swim. If she lost her footing now she would drown. *No, I can't let that happen. I have a promise to keep.*

"Don't even think of it," the man sneered, his gray eyes narrowed, focusing on the girl as though she were prey. "You will never make it."

"What did you do with Zandr?" She struggled to keep her voice from shaking. She was more than outnumbered. In a blink of an eye one of the toads could launch themselves at her, either pinning her down or knock her into the water. Neither result appealed.

Osric chuckled. "Nevermind him. He won't ever be as great as I am. He doesn't have the guts or the power."

Violet's pulse raced. "Did you do something to him? Answer me!"

He took a step towards her. "How sweet. You are concerned for him."

"Of course. He's a friend. Now leave me alone, all of you," she hissed the last part to the toads who were creeping closer.

The female one laughed. "She is quite delightful. I think she would make an adorable wife for my son."

Osric shook his head. "No, she will be mine."

To Violet's horror, fire crackled to life in his hands. She gasped as a glimpse of a memory returned to her. "Fire. You burnt down the fairy village!"

The female toad paled at the accusation. "How could she have remembered that?"

Osric glared at the amphibian, but said nothing to her. Instead he returned his focus to Violet. "Come with me, and I won't harm anyone else. If you don't I will burn down the entire forest where the refugees have taken shelter!"

The threat felt like a stab to Violet's heart as she almost stepped backwards off the lily pad. Fearing for the safety of those who had tried to help her, she realized that she had no choice. She lifted her head as she walked towards her enemies. "You win. I surrender. Just, promise that you will keep your word in not harming them."

"I will… for now."

Chapter 46

Violet glowered down at the white gown she had been forced to wear. She didn't anticipate her surrender would also involve marriage. She was sixteen for crying out loud! Who were they expecting her to wed? Osric? One of the toads? The mole? None of them sat right with her.

Even worse was the pulsing pain that had bloomed in her head since the confrontation on the lily pad. It seemed to increase by the minute. She feared something was wrong with her, but refused to voice it. Perhaps death by whatever was ailing her would be a much better fate than being the wife to whoever the groom was to be. Maybe she would drop dead at the altar saving her from having to say her vows. That would be a blessing in disguise.

She sighed at the sight of the dirt walls and floor of the tiny bedroom she was trapped in. She hated being underground. It felt like a tomb that would be sealed up, never allowing her to see the light of day for as long as she breathed air into her lungs. This wasn't a wedding, but a death sentence. She only wished she knew of a way to achieve freedom without endangering other lives.

Violet gripped the sides of the long skirt longing to scream in despair over her situation until she was hoarse. She didn't want to marry anyone! She wished there was some way for her to escape, yet guarantee that no one would be harmed due to her cowardice. She wrinkled her nose at the thought. She wasn't afraid, she just didn't want to be forced into marriage. It just didn't seem fair to be coerced into doing something as a form of blackmail.

Why did it have to be her anyway? She wasn't anything special. Her appearance she felt was quite plain. She was short, even as… whatever she was. She had nothing of value. So why would anyone want to marry her? Certainly not out of love; they didn't even know her. It made no sense in her head.

Distraught, Violet sank down on the bed. All she wanted to do was curl up into a ball and sleep. However something told her that simple thing would be like giving up. She may have surrendered, but it didn't mean that she wasn't allowed to find another solution to her problem.

She winced as the pain in her skull intensified. Maybe she was dying after all? That would make a very short ending. She felt guilty knowing she wouldn't be able to break the curse or see Zandr ever again. *No. I can't think like that! I will get out of this… somehow.*

Pushing herself to her feet, Violet shoved back the agonizing sensations flooding her head. She'd break the curse if it was the last thing she ever did! The question was, how would she do it, yet keep the fairies safe?

Amber eyes narrowed as she fought to keep focus on the goal at hand. If her destiny was to save the fairies then she would find a way to fulfill it. She couldn't sit around feeling sorry for herself, especially if she was dying. She would have to make the most of what was left of her life the best way she could.

Violet bit her lip as she studied the ceiling. It was all compacted dirt. That meant she might be able to dig herself out. She wasn't sure how much time she had or how far down she was, but it couldn't hurt to try. She glanced around the room in search of something she could use to dig with. She was too short to reach the ceiling by herself, even if she stood on the bed. The only other solution she realized was to dig through a wall and hope she didn't run into any enemies along the way.

Her lips curved into a smirk as she lowered her gaze to the crisp white gown. It was such a shame it was about to get filthy. She was going to enjoy every minute of it.

Chapter 47

A laugh bubbled up in Violet's throat as she glanced down at her now soiled wedding gown. She smeared her dirt-covered hands on the material for a brief moment before continuing to dig. She reveled in the feeling of the cool soil against her skin. It was soothing for some strange reason. She pushed the thought away as she sank her fingers into the earth. It shouldn't be long before she made a hole wide enough to escape through.

The sound of locks clicking made her freeze in terror. She was out of time. Violet squeezed her eyes shut as cold sweat ran down her spine. She held her breath as the door opened.

"Thumbelina! What have you done?" The field mouse scolded from the doorway. She threw up her paws in exasperation. "Your dress is ruined and you are to be married an hour from now."

The strawberry blonde girl choked, startled by the unsettling news. So soon?

The rodent barred her fangs at the girl before a cloud of smoke enveloped the mouse. In her captor's place, stood a regel looking woman with dark red hair and piercing blue eyes clad in a crimson gown.

Violet felt as though her head were about to explode from the extreme burst of pain that ignited in her skull. She fought back the urge to vomit as she sat crouched on the ground. "Mother?"

"Very good, you little snot," the woman laughed. Her amusement was short lived as her lips formed into a scowl as she continued. "If only Vivienne would have given me the sleeping curse like I asked, but no. She had to give it to that child instead! It ruffles my fur just thinking about it. Sometimes I wish I had listened to Idonia about the towers... why am I even telling you all this?"

"I-"

"Oh right. You ruined your dress," she snapped her fingers, and all the dirt had vanished leaving Violet's appearance pristine clean. The wall too had been repaired much to Violet's chagrin. "Try not to make a mess in here again."

"I don't understand. Why are you doing this?"

The woman snorted as she turned on her heel then headed to the door. "Because I can."

"At least tell me who I am marrying."

"The mole."

The door sealed shut before Violet could ask anything more. She pressed her hands to her face as her stomach roiled. Fragments of images spun in her mind making her feel nauseated. That woman was her mother... at least she thought she was. A part of Violet tried to argue against it. She was missing something, but she couldn't figure out what.

"She called me Thumbelina, not Violet," she whispered to herself. The thought struck her as odd, but she'd have to ignore it for now. Her first priority was trying not to get sick as she searched for a way out. The clock was ticking and it was just the matter of time before she was forced to take her vows.

Chapter 48

*V*iolet hugged herself tight. She didn't want to go through with this. She had no desire to marry anyone, let alone a mole of all creatures. Moles lived underground, which meant she would never be able to see the sky again. She had just received the gift of flight and now she must give everything up. She wanted to throw herself onto a bed as she cried tears of grief.

Despite the urge that burned in her gut to mourn what could have been, Violet pushed her thoughts towards finding a way to escape. The room was just dirt and a bed. Using her air magic was a possibility, however, there was no telling how deep down in the earth she was. If fortunate was against her, she could cause a cave in and bury herself alive.

She needed to come up with an idea fast. Time was running out. At least the pain in her head had diminished. She wasn't sure what that meant, but wouldn't focus on it too much. Even though she felt like she were forgetting something important. The idea of having forgotten it was alarming. Did it have to do with the headaches she had been experiencing? The thought of it disturbed her.

Her amber gaze dropped down to her wedding gown, in a desperate attempt to distract herself from the questions circling around in her mind. It was much too long and uncomfortable. Violet wanted to tear it to ribbons with her bare hands. She resisted despite the temptation. She didn't want to face her mother's wrath again.

She's not your mother! A voice in her heart whispered.

Violet ignored it. What difference would it make anyway? She was trapped. She wouldn't be able to fly out of this one. What she needed now was a miracle. She hated the idea of being a damsel in distress. It made her feel so pathetic.

Her heart sank as the woman who she guessed might be a shape-shifter, walked into the room holding a veil.

"It's almost time," the red head grinned.

Violet kept her head high as the lacy material was placed over her head. She wanted to vomit. She felt like she was about to walk to the executioner's block. That fate might have been kinder.

"Don't you look lovely," the woman who she refused to call Mother, cooed.

Violet couldn't find her voice to give a reply. She wasn't sure if she wanted to. The words would not have made the woman very happy. Her mind flitted back to whatever it was that she was trying to remember. The lack of it made her feel empty inside for some reason.

It doesn't matter anymore. This is the beginning of the end.

She knew she would soon wither away.

Chapter 49

*B*reathe. Violet held her head high as she stepped out into the hall holding a bouquet of half-dead flowers. She found them to be rather symbolic to what she was feeling inside. No one could help her now. She had no way out. All she could do was move her feet, one step at a time.

Her eyes widened in horror as she caught sight of her groom. It was Osric. The fairy prince was dressed in his finery—a silk suit of royal blue trimmed in gold. His long hair had been tied back into a ponytail. He looked dashing, but that didn't convince Violet to feel any better about the idea of marriage.

Violet tightened her grip on the flowers. She glanced around the large room, which was empty with the exception of the fairy prince and the red headed woman. "There's no priest?"

"I will wed you two," the woman smiled.

That didn't sit well with Violet. Then she came up with an idea. "Then how will anyone know that the wedding took place? It would be your word against theirs and if Osric wishes to seek the throne…"

The man narrowed his gaze at her. "What are you trying to suggest?"

"Why would you want to marry in a dank hole in the ground when you could have a royal wedding? It would express your power and worth. Hundreds of eyes would be on you, captivated by your magmatic nature, staring in sheer awe." Violet lifted her arms, emphasizing her words as she struggled to convince him that he was making a mistake in having a secluded wedding. "It would be the event of the century!"

"Osric, there is no time-" the woman began to protest.

"Silence!" He snapped a hand out. "There is always time. My dear bride to be has a very good point. Why should I marry here like some sort of an animal? It denies me my honored birthright as the future ruler of the Fairy Kingdom!"

Violet nodded. She would pretend to go along with the wedding as long as it got her to the surface. From there she could make her escape. She just hoped her plan worked.

"But we agreed-" the woman began only to be cut off.

"I am royalty!" Osric shouted. "No one is going to tell me what to do. Not you, not my parents, or my worthless siblings. It is I who should inherent the throne, not them! We shall return to the surface and take the kingdom by force if we have to. I shall have what belongs to me!"

Violet remained quiet. She didn't want to start a war, but she didn't want to marry the selfish, pompous prince either. She'd find a way to protect the kingdom and escape. Somehow.

Chapter 50

Violet bit the inside of her cheek to keep from grinning at the sight of the sky. How she missed the warm embrace of the sunlight and the gentle kisses of a cool breeze brushing against her skin. It made her feel homesick even though she hadn't been trapped underground for even a full day.

If she could make it a few more feet then she would be able to try using her air magic to shove her would-be-groom and fake mother away so she could flee. She just had to be patient.

Just as she was preparing to make a break for it, a large cloud of what resembled smoke burst to life, blinding them.

"Thumbelina! Where are you?" The red head yelled, groping at the air for the small girl.

"Who is behind this?" The elder fairy prince growled, "I will kill you!"

As Violet drew back in fear, a pair of arms wrapped around, lifting her from the ground. Before she could scream, a hand clapped over her mouth. She was about to bite them when a familiar voice whispered in her ear, "Relax, it's me."

Zandr. Violet wasn't sure why those simple words seemed to put her at ease, but if he could get her out of her marriage, she wasn't about to argue. Instead she nodded, staying quiet so Osric and the woman couldn't find her. She ignored their calls as Zandr took her by the arm and led her out of the smoke. Once they were far enough away, he lifted her up before taking off to the sky.

"How did you find me?" the girl inquired, still bewildered to have been freed from her captors. "I mean, I was planning on escaping on my own, but well, thanks."

The fairy prince shrugged as he set her down on a tree branch. "It wasn't easy. After I awoke, I noticed that the dirt that was left behind was from the caverns near the waterfall so that was where I headed first. By some luck or miracle, there you were."

Violet raised her eyebrows in surprise. "You recognized the dirt?"

"It shimmers," he explained, holding out a handful. I used to play there when I was a child, along with my siblings. I didn't recognize it right away when I first saw you. I feel like a fool for not realizing it sooner. My brother really has turned against us."

"I thought you didn't believe me."

"I saw him before I passed out. At first I thought it was a dream or some strange hallucination. I still don't quite understand what to make of it all except that… he's become my enemy."

"He was going to make me to marry him. I had to trick him outside so that I could use my magic to escape. Then you appeared." Violet frowned as she looked into Zandr's silvery eyes. "Why did you save me? I know I'm supposed to break the curse, but Osric is your brother. My marrying him shouldn't have mattered."

Zandr raised an eyebrow at her. "Did you desire to wed him?"

"No-"

"Then this is a pointless argument." As she was about to protest, he whirled on her. "You were being forced into something you didn't want to do. I could see the misery on your face as you trailed after them. I could tell that something was wrong."

Violet stared at him for a good long moment. Then something struck her. Did Zandr like her? She wasn't sure how she felt about that. At least he didn't pressure her into anything, unlike his brother. She just hoped that he didn't have the same expectations running through his head. "So, now what?"

"We do what we said we were going to—complete your quest."

Chapter 51

Amber eyes darted around the tall grasses in anticipation of her kidnappers ambushing them again. She didn't want to be forced back underground, much less get married to someone she didn't care for. She refused!

"Are you all right?"

Her head snapped up at Zandr's voice. A blush tinted her cheeks as she glanced up at his puzzled expression. "Yes, why do you ask?"

"You keep making strange faces."

"I have?" Violet winced as the exclamation came out in a squeak of surprise. She lowered her head in embarrassment. "I'm just worried that your brother and that woman would attack again. There is something about her that is... unsettling, but I can't put my finger on what."

"Perhaps something to do with your past?"

"Maybe." She sighed, growing more frustrated with the whole situation. It was one thing to be chosen to break a curse, it was a completely different thing to be forced into an unwanted marriage. "I wish I knew why they want me so much. I doubt he's in love with me. There has to be more to it..."

Zandr fell silent as they continued their journey back to the castle.

"It just isn't fair. I didn't ask for this. I'm not even sure if I am Thumbelina like everyone insists I am. I don't even know how to break curses," she continued ranting.

"Poor baby. You'd rather cry over yourself than the fact that if the curse isn't broken that we will all be eaten by locusts."

"What?" Violet stopped dead in her tracks, stunned by Zandr's cool words. That was the first time she had heard this.

"You heard me."

"But…" She growled under her breath then kicked at the ground. "Why does it have to be me?"

Zandr spun around to face her, his expression no longer gentle. "I have no idea what my imbecile of a brother is playing at. The fact that he thinks he can steal away the only person that can save us from certain death is absurd. However, if you think fate is cruel, wait until the forest is invaded by insects that will tear you limb from limb. Because without the birds, we are all doomed. So stop your whining and take responsibility! This isn't just about you."

Violet stared at him, horrified. She didn't know what to say except a whispered, "I'm sorry."

He glared at her, as he nodded. "I will accept your apology once you stop being selfish. There are lives at stake in this. I will state just as much to my older brother if he ever dares to show his face again. This isn't a child's game. This is life and death."

She wanted to argue, but was afraid she might instead burst into tears the moment she opened her mouth. Instead she bopped her head in acknowledgement of Zandr's words. She didn't think she was being selfish, she just didn't like the fact that she was being forced into something she didn't ask for. It didn't seem right considering she still lacked the memories to tell her otherwise. It was very disconcerting.

"We're wasting valuable time," he growled, spinning back around on his heel.

Violet took a step to keep up with him then tripped over the long skirt of her wedding gown. In aggravation she beat her fists on the ground. "Stupid dress!"

"Stand up."

"I didn't fall on purpose if that's what you're thinking."

He narrowed his eyes as he hauled her to her feet then withdrew a dagger. With a few quick slashes, he trimmed the excess length off. "The pink one was much better."

"I didn't ask to wear this."

"I never said you did. The pink one suited you more." He sheathed the blade then sighed. "Look, I'm not trying to be mean. There is just a lot at stake and very little time left. By tomorrow morning, the forest with be overridden with locusts."

Violet scowled. "Is that why there aren't that many insects and animals around?"

"Yes. Their instincts are telling them to run. We should be doing the same, but... there isn't anywhere to go." Zandr ran a hand down his face. "Once this forest is demolished, they will move onto the next. We need the birds to return. That's even more important than being given back the ability to change our size."

"Why didn't you tell me this sooner?"

"I didn't want to scare everyone. Only a few people know. My parents included. That's why I'm so infuriated by my brother. He should know better!"

Violet had no idea of what to say as Zandr let his frustrations boil over. "I don't know what he is planning either, but I promise to do my best to break the curse at whatever costs. You have my word."

The prince stilled as though unaware that she was still listening to him. "Now I'm being the bully. Look, I understand that you didn't ask for this, however, we need you. I will find a way to make it up to you somehow."

"We'll worry about that later. How's your energy?"

"Good, why?"

"Then let's fly. Like you said, the clock is ticking."

He nodded as with a flash of light his silver wings appeared.

Violet felt her lips curve in a smile as she called out hers as well. It was time for her to face reality and do what she was meant to—break the curse. After all she may feel like she had the weight of the world on her shoulders, however, she was the only one that could break the insidious curse that had wreaked havoc throughout the fairylands. Despite the daunting task she would strive to fulfill her duty as the Chosen of the Crystal Garden.

Chapter 52

It didn't take long before Violet and Zandr were landing in front of the caves. She shivered as she glanced into the dark caverns. "Maybe it would be best to look for the Sky Fortress ourselves."

"We don't know how to find it. The wise woman will be able to provide us with some clues."

Butterflies fluttered in Violet's stomach as she peered into their destination. She felt uneasy about treading into a place so far away from the light. Something about it put her on edge. "I don't know about this. It's seems like a bad idea to me. How do you know if she can be trusted?"

"She hasn't steered us wrong yet." Zandr scowled as Violet continued to resist. "Must you be so stubborn?"

"I was just abducted! Of course, I'm going to be suspicious. Can you blame me?" She shoved at her strawberry blonde curls as the anxiety refused to let up. "I would feel better if she met us here on the surface. I don't like the idea of being trapped again."

"I will keep you safe."

Violet's stomach did flip flops at the earnest tone of Zandr's words. What was going on with her?

Zandr took her hand forcing her to look at him. "I'm going to stay with you for as long as you need me. You are not expected to take on this quest alone."

"Okay." Violet felt herself go dreamy at the gesture. Could it be? Did she like him in the non-friendship terms? It seemed incredible for her to think that she was falling for a guy she barely knew who on top of that was royalty! It couldn't be true. It had to be all her imagination or part of the curse, anything, but love! Did she really just now think the 'L' word? Oh no... This was not happening. This was pure insanity! She must be losing her mind if she was even considering... that word. She would just ignore it. That was the only logical way to deal with whatever it was.

She felt a blush creeping to her cheeks. Why couldn't she get her mind off him? This wasn't like her. She drew a deep breath, struggling to focus. Easier said than done. Why wasn't her brain cooperating? This was madness! She had known him for less than a day.

Violet closed her eyes trying in desperation to find some semblance of sanity somewhere in that head of hers. Maybe it was just a simple crush. He was a good looking guy after all. Who in their right mind wouldn't fall head over heels for him? She had to stop thinking about the fairy prince. It was going to kill her if she continued.

Think about something else! Violet gritted her teeth. It wasn't working out so well. She wanted to act like everything was normal, but now... it was difficult. One part of her didn't want to give in while another... She refused to let that side have a voice. It was all just too baffling.

"Are you all right?"

"Fine!" Her face turned bright red at her outburst. She pulled her hand out of Zandr's, surprised at having snapped at him. "Sorry... I'm just stressed out. I'll be okay."

His brows knit together, but he let it go. "If you say so. Do you wish to meet the wise woman or not?"

"Why not. We are running out of options after all," Violet sighed. The bubbly feeling had left her as a sensation of dread stirred in her belly. She just hoped that her nerves would be proven wrong. She allowed Zandr to escort her through the mouth of the cave. As he made it through the threshold however, the floor gave way beneath him to her horror, sending him into the inky black below.

Chapter 53

"Zandr!" Violet's heart hammered in her chest as she stared down into the gaping hole where the fairy prince had once stood. Fear raced through her mind as tears stung her amber eyes. What was she going to do? What if he had just fallen to his death? A part of her was afraid that she would never see him again. A tightening sensation filled her chest at that very thought. Worried, she peered over the edge. "Zandr? Can you hear me? Are you okay? Say something!"

"I'm fine. No need to worry," he yelled back much to her relief.

"Do you need any help? I could fly down-"

"No! I'll be right up. Just give me a moment… I need to get my bearings."

Violet made herself step back a few feet. She was concerned over his wellbeing, but didn't want to risk causing more of the ground to collapse, potentially burying him alive. She was just grateful that he was okay.

A few minutes later the fairy prince emerged covered in dirt, yet alive. Violet rushed to him, anxious to verify for herself that he was indeed all right. She looked him over, but didn't see any wounds. "You're not hurt, are you?"

Zandr shook his head, as he landed beside her. His silver wings disappeared as he began dusting himself off. "We should keep going. We are running out of time after all."

"What if more of the floor caves in? It could be dangerous. Maybe we should find another way to the wise woman. She wouldn't want us to risk our lives after all."

He took her hand, reassuring her. "We'll be fine. Don't worry so much."

Violet frowned, but dropped the subject as he led her towards the walls of the cavern, away from the gaping hole. Arguing seemed pointless. After all, time was valuable. It wouldn't be right to waste it on pettiness. Instead she bit her tongue, ignoring the urge to protest. "If you're sure."

"I am."

She glanced over her shoulder at the light for a moment then refocused on the darkness of the cave. She hoped that they wouldn't have to spend too much time hidden from the surface. It seemed like the more time she spent away from seeing the sky, the more restless she became. The sooner the curse was broken, the better off they all would be.

Chapter 54

*T*he caverns were immense. The stalactites seemed to jut out from the dark heavens as the travelers wove around the humungous stalagmites piercing up from the ground. For once, Violet was glad to be so small. The risk of being impaled was far less than if she was human-sized. If the ceiling were to come down, she might have a better chance of dodging out of the path of danger. Then of course, were her newfound powers. She was still unsure of how she made them work. Perhaps if she ever got her memories back she would find out the truth.

"How much further?" She looked at Zandr as she asked the question. She still couldn't determine what her true feelings were regarding him. It was unnerving that she would even consider the idea of liking him, but there it was. That did not, however, mean that he would consider the same of her. As far as she knew, they were platonic companions with the sole goal of breaking the curse the single thing that they had in common.

"She shouldn't be too far…" Zandr's brow knit in confusion as he glanced around the caverns.

"Good." Violet's stomach churned with unease. She ignored it, chalking it up to being nothing more than nerves. She would be fine. Zandr would see to it. She wasn't alone in this. Something darted in shadows out of the corner of her eye sending shivers down her spine. "What was that?"

"What?"

Violet's heart lurched as warning bells began to go off in her head. "Something was moving."

"It was just your imagination."

"No, it wasn't. I know what I saw," Violet frowned at the fairy prince, annoyed at having been called delusional. "I don't like it here. Maybe we'll have better luck finding the Sky Fortress on our own. It can't be that hard-"

Zandr grabbed the girl's arm before she could bolt. "No, we need to stay here."

"I don't understand. Why-" She frowned as his grip tightened to the point where she was certain he would leave bruises. "Ease up a bit. You're hurting me!"

The fairy prince gave a deep menacing chuckle as the shadows closed in around them. Before Violet realized what had happened, she found herself surrounded by Woodlins. She spun towards Zandr then froze in shock. Rather finding herself gazing up at the silver eyed prince, she instead stared horrified into sneering face of the Woodlin Queen.

Chapter 55

*V*iolet choked on a scream. How could this be happening to her? Was it all some elaborate scheme? Did Zandr even exist or was he the Woodlin Queen the whole time? Confusion swirled in her head making her nauseated as she tried to make sense of everything. "What is going on? Who are you?"

"Foolish child. I'm disappointed in how dense you are." The queen laughed as she flung the girl to her minions.

Violet shrieked as she was caught and held upright, her arms pinned by several clawed hands that dug into her flesh. She bit back a pained cry. Instead she raised her head, directing her attention to her nemesis. "Forgive me if I lack the memories to come up with a proper retort. I suppose you're about to tell me that everything is a lie, correct?"

"My how you amuse me. It's almost a shame I can't keep you as a pet any longer. I have enjoyed our little games," the queen taunted.

"You... you're the shape-shifter!"

"And here I thought you were denser than a brick. It's nice to be proven wrong once in a while. Did you enjoy my little fabrications? I worked very hard on making them just right."

Something in Violet seemed to snap. The woman had been toying with her. She was tired of being used for whatever convince others found in her. She was no one's plaything. Amber eyes narrowed in outrage as Violet struggled against the minions' hold. "I do not appreciate being treated like some sort of a plaything. I suppose you are going to tell me that Zandr is a fake as well as everything else in this world."

"Now you are disappointing me again. Pity. I was starting to have higher expectations in you. Oh well." The shape-shifter snorted. "No, that sad excuse of a prince is real and very annoying to boot."

Violet filed that little factoid away in her mind. That meant that at some point Zandr must have gotten captured. She refused to even consider of the possibility of him being dead. "So, how did you take his place? I doubt he volunteered."

"Aren't you fond of asking questions..."

"I don't have anything better to do," the girl shrugged, "I might as well make use of my time in some form. So, are you going to tell me or would you rather have a staring contest instead?"

The shape-shifter snorted. "Aren't we demanding?"

"No, just bored. It's not like I can go anywhere. You have me in your clutches."

Just as the woman was about to oblige, a fiery inferno surrounded her. She screamed in agony as the flames snaked up her body. The Woodlins charged at the fire in a desperate effort to save their queen only to find themselves engulfed in the same fierce blaze. Violet watched in horror as her enemies burned.

"I find her smugness tiresome," a deep voice scoffed from behind her.

Violet turned then gaped in shock as Osric strutted towards her. "You…"

He ran a hand through his rich, dark hair. "Who did you think was the real puppet master? Hello, my bride to be. Did you miss me?"

Chapter 56

"You killed them! You didn't even give them a chance." Violet's heart pounded in her chest as she backed away from the fairy prince.

"They deserved it. After all, they had stolen what is mine."

"I am not yours. I am no one's possession." Violet glared at him, her rage growing. A warming sensation flooded her body as a silver bow etched with butterflies formed in her hands. Without questioning it, she raised the weapon, pointing it at him. "Leave me be or I will retaliate."

Osric laughed. "You don't even have any arrows. What are you going to do, wing air at me?"

"How about dealing with me instead," a familiar voice growled from behind Violet.

"Brother! How good of you to join us," the elder prince greeted Zandr.

"I don't know you anymore. You've become a monster. What has happened to you?" The silver-eyed fairy prince drew a dagger as he joined Violet's side. "You killed without mercy."

Osric snorted at the proclamation. "They deserved it. That... thing thought she was my superior. She was *dead* wrong. No one shall be above me."

Zandr tightened his grip on his weapon. "I don't care how you feel about the kingdom. Our older brothers have been groomed to take over the throne. Ryin is already married and has a child on the way. We are not meant to rule."

"You are so naïve, little brother."

"And you are so egotistical. When are you going to stop thinking about yourself for a change? You could do great good without being king. Instead, you have thrown all that potential away by turning your back on your people!"

"They were never mine to begin with," Osric stated with a snort.

Zandr shook his head. "That's where you are wrong. What we do as royals is supposed to be for the people, not ourselves. You have lost your way if you think otherwise. We are here to help not hinder. We are meant to lead whether we are king or prince. The people look to us to show them the way. You are not capable of that anymore."

"You are blinded. As ruler you decided how to treat those around you."

"You're a fool, Osric." Zandr looked at his older brother in disgust. "Who do you think you are? How could you do this?"

"I am the rightful heir."

"You are an imbecile."

"You know nothing, little brother. You have never tasted power before."

"If it means becoming a traitor like you then no thanks."

Osric chuckled. "You are amusing. The only fool here is you."

Zandr's eyes narrowed with fury. "You destroyed a town with your fire magic. I know it was you. Why did you do it?"

Osric shrugged. "They were disrespectful and had to pay."

A burst of flames exploded in front of the two brothers. Zandr shielded Violet as Osric drew back in surprise.

"I have to disagree," a female voice hissed as the fire diminished to smoke. Inhuman blue eyes glowed through the haze. "The biggest imbecile is you, Osric. How dare you use the magic I taught you to kill me. You shall pay dearly for your misguided stupidity."

Violet stared in bewilderment as the form of the shape-shifter appeared before them. Things just went from bad to worse.

Chapter 57

The shape-shifter changed her appearance to that of the red haired woman. She smirked at the look of unadulterated hatred that shone on Osric's face. "The student should never try to best the teacher."

"You taught him magic?" Zandr inquired, his voice tinged with awe and horror.

"He was tired of being useless so we made a pact. Of course it seems I got the bad end of the deal. That will be an easy fix."

Violet opened her mouth before she could reconsider speaking. "Do you mean... was I supposed to be some sort of prize? Is that why you wanted me?"

The red head laughed. "Little do you know, child. He was just supposed to keep you... contained. Nothing more."

The elder fairy prince glared at the shape-shifter. "How dare you speak such lies, witch. I was never useless-"

"Please. You are third in line for the throne and slipping even further down. You and your brother here are mere afterthoughts. You will never be kings." She examined her fingernails then snickered. "I gave you a chance to be something great, but you were far too immature to accept such a great responsibility. Now I must go back to the drawing board in dealing with our little… nuisance."

Zandr angled himself between the woman and Violet. "I will not let you touch her. Leave us be or I shall destroy you."

"You can do nothing to me."

Violet broke out of her stupor enough to raise her bow, aiming it at the shape-shifter. She refused to be controlled any longer. "Maybe he can't, but I can. That's why you decided to have me married off. You fear me. You know that I can ruin whatever schemes you have plotted. I'm right, aren't I? Just try to deny it."

"You wish," the woman snorted.

"We shall see about that." A glowing arrow appeared as Violet pulled back on the string of her weapon. She didn't say a word as she sent the projectile loose. It whizzed past the shape-shifter, narrowly missing both her and Osric.

"Watch it! You could have hit me, you miserable little brat," the elder fairy prince growled.

The shape-shifter laughed. "I see you have found your flower. Well, this has gotten interesting indeed."

Violet narrowed her gaze as she tightened her grip on the bow. "I've had my rose for some time now. You were just too full of yourself to figure it out!"

"Then I'll just have to eliminate you."

Before Violet could react, she found herself encircled by a wall of flames. She looked back at Zandr, fearful that he had been harmed.

"Thumbelina!"

She gasped as a burst of black flooded her vision, then all went silent.

Chapter 58

"*Y*ou really shouldn't have mocked her," a soft voice scolded.

Violet groaned as she rubbed her eyes then blinked at the sight of a golden blonde haired girl dressed in a lavender gown. "Who... How?"

"You're safe. At least for now."

"I feel like I know you..."

"You do. My name is Lunette. We have met before, although you don't seem to have the memories on those encounters any longer."

Violet frowned at the sight of the ocean. She was sitting on a beach near a large ship. "How did I get here?"

"You're not actually here. This is all in your mind," a second voice explained as two girls stepped out of the shadows of the ship. The one who had spoken had auburn hair and striking hazel eyes. The other one was shorter with long white blonde hair and bright blue eyes. She gave Violet a small smile, but said nothing.

"How is that even possible? Does this have to do with the Crystal Garden?"

"Yes," Lunette replied. "We are all connected. Those of us who are present haven't fulfilled their quest yet. The time for yours is running out so you must make haste."

"The curse," Violet said, recalling her mission. "How can I break it? I don't know the first thing about magic."

"Listen to your heart. Let it be your guide."

"What do you mean? I still don't understand," she said, confused over Lunette's words. As she walked towards the blonde girl, everything around her vanished. Instead she found herself back in the Crystal Garden.

"It's not going to be easy," Grace murmured from behind her. She brushed a hand over the Air pedestal. "It never is."

Violet sighed in despair. "I just want things to start making sense! No one is giving me any answers. It's getting really aggravating trying to understand all the cryptic things everyone is telling me. Can I please have a straight answer?"

"There you go whining again. I think I liked you better smarting off to the witch." The blonde rolled her eyes. "This is part of your quest. You have to find your own way, just make sure you are prepared to make certain sacrifices, if the occasion calls for it."

"Like what?"

Grace shook her head. "I cannot tell you. You have to decide what is worth giving up to break the curse. Only then will you find your answers. Take great care in your decision. If I had done so with mine, then I wouldn't be here right now."

Violet pursed her lips as she studied the guardian. "What happened?"

"I didn't listen to my instincts and instead jumped to the wrong conclusion. Nevermind my misfortune, you still have time to fix yours."

"Why are you being nicer to me?"

Grace's lips curved into a smile. "Because you are showing strength you didn't exhibit before. Don't give up, no matter what."

A white fog swirled around Violet as she lost sight of Grace. She wanted to ask more, but made a silent promise to keep the words she had been told to heart.

Chapter 59

A gasp escaped Violet's throat as she found herself surrounded by hot flames. Without thinking of it, she used a combination of her air magic and the loose dirt to smother the fire. She didn't question what she had just done. Instead she looked at Zandr, who had tried to shield her from danger when she had passed out. His clothing and face was covered in soot, but he didn't seem to be injured.

"Are you all right?" She inquired, after realizing that they had been left alone in the inferno. There was no sign of the shape-shifter or Osric.

Zandr pulled her into a shaky hug. "I wasn't sure if you would ever wake up."

Violet frowned, but accepted the embrace as she wrapped her arms around him, relieved that he seemed to indeed be okay. "How long was I out?"

"Not long. The witch seemed surprised though. I didn't expect her to leave us here or at least you. She took my brother then left."

"They must have gone to the Sky Fortress."

He nodded, pulling away from the strawberry blonde haired girl. "That was my thought too."

Violet bit her lip. She wasn't sure what to make of Zandr hugging her. Perhaps it was just something fairies did? She decided not to worry about it... for now.

Rising to her feet, Violet glanced around the cavern then made a face at her dress. What had once been pristine white was now a dingy gray. She smiled in satisfaction at having ruined the wedding gown. It was quite appropriate since she had no desire to get married anyway. "So, any idea on where to find the Sky Fortress?"

"No, sorry."

"It's all right. We'll figure something out," she smiled, despite feeling distraught over having no set path to her destination. With her two enemies in the same location as the place where she had to go to break the curse, Violet suspected that her mission had just doubled, if not tripled in difficulty. She wouldn't let that deter her however. She needed to complete her quest no matter the consequences.

Zandr nodded, "Let's just get out of here first. I don't want to take a chance that there might be booby traps around."

"You won't hear any arguments from me."

She allowed Zandr to take her hand as he led her out of the cave while she racked her brain for their next course of action.

Chapter 60

Violet released a sigh of relief at seeing the sky once again. She didn't think she was claustrophobic, but the longer she was away from the fresh air and warm sunlight, the more anxious she felt.

"It's good to be away from that place," Zandr commented from her side.

"Yes, although I will admit, that being underground is much worse."

"Fairies aren't meant to live underground."

"I'm not a fairy," she said in a whisper. Something about admitting that little fact hurt her deep down although she didn't understand why.

Zandr shook his head. "Maybe, but you do have wings. You don't belong below the surface either."

Violet looked at him for a moment. She wasn't sure if there was any hidden meaning in his words, however, now was not the time to ask. "We need to find the Sky Fortress."

"Right."

"I suppose the best way to do so is to search for a cloud that appears as though it's on fire," she scowled as she lifted her head up. This was going to be far more difficult than she would ever imagine it to be.

"They couldn't have gone far."

She twisted a curl around with her fingertips. "We should go someplace high. That will give us a better advantage. What is the tallest structure?"

The fairy prince pointed behind them. "The mountain peak. It's the best answer I can come up with."

"And it's not far from the cave... Zandr, you're a genius!" Violet grinned, happy to have a good lead for a change. "The cloud must be close to the top of the mountain. We better hurry before that witch relocates."

"The most expedient way would be to fly."

"Then let's not waste any more time," Violet's iridescent wings appeared on her back the same time Zandr's silver ones did. They exchanged brief glances before taking off into the sky.

Chapter 61

*I*t took little time to reach the mountain peak. Violet shivered at the drop of temperature as she perched on a snow covered tree branch. She didn't think she had ever been so high up before. It was somewhat exhilarating, yet frightening at the same time.

"Are you all right?" Zandr inquired from her side. "You didn't use up too much energy, did you?"

His concern caused her face to flush. She pushed back a lock of hair from her face hoping he didn't notice her reddening cheeks. "I don't think so. What about you?"

"I need to catch my breath a little longer, but I haven't reached my limit."

"That's good," Violet nodded, inwardly cringing at how awkward she was beginning to feel. She wondered if lacking her memories had anything to do with it. "I don't mind waiting."

Zandr leaned back against the tree trunk. He stared up at the sky for several minutes before speaking again. "I know that dealing with the witch and Osric is something you would rather not do. I just want to say that I find it admirable that you are willing to fight for us in breaking the curse despite this not being your war."

"But it is. I realize that it may not seem like it, however, I am stuck in the middle just like everyone else. I may not have my memories, but the shape-shifter… we seem to have a past although I'm not sure what it entails." She scrunched her nose in distaste over not being able to remember. "I'm not doing this for just me. I'm doing this for everyone."

"I'm glad to know that I have put my trust into someone worthy."

Violet didn't know how to respond to that. Instead she tucked a loose curl behind her ear. "I'm just doing what anyone else would do."

Zandr shook his head. "No, I thought you were selfish before, but you've proved me wrong. You're not who I thought you were."

She sighed. "This might not be the real me. I might be someone different with my memories."

"I disagree. Memories can shape us, however, without them we act through our hearts instead. This is the real you."

She stared at the fairy prince in bewilderment. Why was he talking so earnest to her all of a sudden? Before he seemed so focused on breaking the curse. Now… she was getting rather confused. "Why are you telling me this?"

"Because you're unique. You have this inner strength that I could never have imagined. Not when I first met you." Zandr paused as though gathering his thoughts. "The point is, I have faith that you will succeed in breaking the curse."

Violet didn't know what to say. Instead she turned her attention to the sky, then frowned. Hovering above the Whisper Falls Castle was a large red tinged cloud. Her heart thudded in her chest at the discovery. "I think I found it."

Zandr rose to his feet and looked to where she was pointing. His lips curved into a half smile. "Then let's pay the witch and my disgrace of a brother a visit."

Chapter 62

*V*iolet struggled to keep her concentration as she flew towards the large cloud. The air was getting thinner, making her feel short of breath. Zandr managed to keep pace with her much to her relief. She was glad she wouldn't have to go alone.

"Just a bit further. We can do this," he encouraged.

"Right." She gritted her teeth, forcing herself to keep focused on reaching the fortress. She couldn't risk failing. Not now. Not when she was so close. In the back of her mind she wondered if she would be able to stand on a cloud. She guessed she would find out soon enough.

It wasn't long before they reached their destination. Violet puzzled over the fact that the cloud seemed to maintain their weight.

Zandr narrowed his silver eyes at what should have been nothing more than vapor. "I wonder if a spell had been cast to allow the fortress to stay afloat."

"Your guess is as good as mine." Butterflies swarmed her stomach as she lifted her gaze to the Sky Fortress. It was a massive structure with tall spires that reached for the heavens. The place seemed rather foreboding with its dark stonework. Violet shuddered to think of how they would go about sneaking into such a place without being caught.

"I guess now that we're here, we need to find a way in," the fairy prince murmured. "I doubt they will welcome us with open arms."

"I suppose not."

The pair exchanged glances then turned back to face the fortress.

"Any ideas?" Violet inquired.

Zandr shook his head. "I'm afraid not."

"Great."

"We shall come up with some sort of plan."

Violet twisted a curl around her finger in thought. She urged herself to think, but so far continued to come up blank. "Strategy is not my strong suit!"

Zandr put a hand on her shoulder. "Stay calm. It will come to one of us."

She drew a deep breath then exhaled as she closed her eyes. Then it hit her. "We can try flying to the top of the fortress. From there we should be able to locate a door that will lead us inside. The only potential problem is whether or not it's locked."

He nodded. "Sounds like a good start at least. Let's try it."

Chapter 63

Violet pursed her lips in surprise at having not encountered any guards at the Sky Fortress. Could she be wrong about where she needed to go to break the curse? It was too late to turn back now. At least she was correct about there being a door on the roof.

"So far so good," Zandr commented as they crept towards the lone door.

"I guess it's now or never." Violet's hand shook as she reached for the handle. She anticipated it flying open as someone grabbed her, dragging her inside before she could even scream. What she got instead was an unlocked door that squeaked as she opened it. "Odd."

"Maybe they expected us to use the front?" Zandr scratched the back of his head in speculation.

"I'm just hoping that this isn't a trap."

He touched her arm in a reassuring gesture. "You are not alone this time. I'll have your back."

She gave a half smile then stepped through the threshold. It was darker inside than she imagined. She couldn't see a single sign of a burning candle or torch anywhere. Her nerves jittered as though she were being electrocuted, but she continued on. For some reason she felt better having Zandr with her. Plus, it was a fortress in the sky that she was infiltrating, not a hole in the ground.

Violet bit her lip as she came to fork in the middle of the corridor. Three directions to choose from. Only one was the one she needed. She hated being forced to make a quick decision. She was tempted to close her eyes and spin around, stopping at random in one of the directions, but figured that Zandr might frown upon such an irresponsible way of handling of the situation. "I'm not sure which way is the right one."

The fairy prince's brow knitted together at he looked at their options. "We will have to choose one and cross our fingers we picked the correct one."

That seemed simple enough. Violet knew she was going to be disappointed in herself if she took them in the wrong direction however. After much debate she went right. She held her breath as she walked down the hallway. So far, no alarm bells seemed to go off in her head. It wasn't until they reached the end of the corridor did a bad feeling stir in her belly.

"Is something the matter?" Zandr glanced down at her in concern.

Before she could reply, a bright light bloomed to life around them, blinding them.

The last thing Violet remembered was laughter before all fell silent.

Chapter 64

*A*mber eyes fluttered open then blinked in surprise. What was she doing in bed? Violet sat up as she glanced around the bedroom in confusion. Something didn't feel right. She lowered her gaze and scowled at seeing her gray school uniform. Did she fall asleep in her clothes? She didn't remember even walking into her room let alone lying down on her bed.

Bemusement washed over her as she let her gaze wander. There was something she had to do. What was it? Violet growled in frustration. Her mind refused to cooperate. Instead she was left with one big blank. It was enough to drive a person insane!

A knocking at her door interrupted her thoughts. "Violet, dinner is ready. Come down and eat."

Her mother? The teenaged girl rubbed her face as a mild pain pulsed through her head. No it couldn't be… could it? She was getting so agitated that she wanted to scream.

"Violet!" The woman was shouting her name again.

"This isn't right," the strawberry blonde haired girl murmured to herself. "I'm not supposed to be here."

She cried out in alarm as the bedroom door rattled.

"Young lady, come downstairs this instant!"

Violet squeezed her eyes shut in a desperate attempt to wake herself up. She paled as she realized that it wasn't working. Either this was an intense dream or something else.

Not wanting to find out what might be in store for her outside the door, she went to the window instead. She was two stories up. For an odd reason that didn't seem to scare her. She unlatched the locks on the window and sat on the ledge. She could see green grass and several bushes below. Without a second's hesitation she jumped.

"What?" Violet cried out startled at finding herself on a bed in an underground tunnel. A cold sweat broke out down her back. This couldn't be possible. She jumped out of a window! How could she be underground? It didn't make sense.

"Thumbelina, you're finally awake!" A field mouse chirped as she entered the room.

"Get away from me!" Violet bolted to the opposite side of the room as far from the rodent as possible. She clenched her hands into fists. "You did something to me, didn't you? You messed up my mind. I want out of here this instant!"

"Child, calm down. You must be delirious with fever-"

"I'm not sick," she snapped, fury radiating from her amber eyes. "Fix whatever you did to me or so help me I shall make you pay. I am tired of being manipulated like some sort of doll. I am not your plaything."

The mouse chuckled as a dark smoke surrounded her, revealing a striking red headed woman with cold blue eyes. "I see I have estimated the power of my elixir accurately. This is very troublesome."

"I know who you are... You tried to erase that little fact-" Before Violet could finish her sentence, the world around her dissolved. The next thing she knew she was surrounded by people, their loud chatter mixing with the music in the background.

"Violet."

Her head snapped up in shock. She gaped at the young man dressed in a tuxedo by her side. His intense green eyes bore into her. It was then she realized that she was dressed in a shimmery silver dress with strappy high heels. "How did I get here?"

The young man snorted as he ran a hand through his perfectly coiffed blonde hair. "I brought you in my limo. Don't you remember?"

Violet shook her head as she back away from him. "No, that's not right. I wasn't here a moment ago."

He raised an eyebrow at her. "Are you on something?"

Rather than reply, she darted her eyes around the room. "I've got to get out of here. This is not where I'm supposed to be."

"Violet-"

"No!" She slapped his hand away as he reached out to grab her then bolted towards the door of the gymnasium. Without a second's glance back she made it through the door and to the stairs. However, just as she set one foot on the waxed surface, she caught her heel on the edge, and pitched forward. She squeezed her eyes shut as she braced for impact.

Chapter 65

*V*iolet opened her eyes then blinked. Rather than having broken her neck in a tumble down the stairs, she was floating above them on a pillow of air. Despite it being a strange turn of events, she was grateful to have been spared the pain and potential death that would have followed her fall.

"That's right. I am the Chosen of the Air Crystal Rose... I remember now. I'm Thumbelina."

The world around her cracked before shattering in what sounded like an explosion of glass. In its place was a cold stone room. Standing in the middle was the shape-shifter glaring daggers at the girl. "You miserable little brat! You broke my illusions. Do you even know how hard they were to create? How much hard work it took to craft each one to suit your mind?"

Violet dropped down to the ground, undeterred by the woman's insults. Without a thought, she materialized her bow in her hand. "You should have known better than to be able to cage me in my mind forever. That was foolish on your part. Now, tell me where is Zandr."

"He's indisposed."

"If you have done him any harm..."

"You will what?" the shape-shifter challenged.

A strong wind whirled around them as Violet stared at her enemy. In a blink of an eye the ruined wedding gown had turned back into the pink dress Violet wore upon receiving her crystal rose. Her pink lips curved into a smile as she raised her bow. "Much better. Now, if you have a desire to fight me, then so be it. Just know that I will not hold back. Plus, I can extinguish your fire magic."

"Your powers are weak compared to mine. I can tear you to shreds with a single thought."

"You killed my mother. Don't even try to deny it. I know it was you. How else were you going to be able to keep me under your thumb then take her place in my mind?" The accusation came out in a whisper as Violet remained frozen in place. She wanted to have the element of surprise at hand. "Enough games. Tell me what I want to know or else you forfeit your life."

The woman snorted. "Are you going to kill me? Is that the solution?"

"Forfeit does not mean death. I'm sure a prison would suit you just fine."

The red head cackled. "Now who is the foolish one?"

Violet didn't even bother to dodge the fireball that was launched her way. She just caught it with a blanket of wind then smothered it. "You can't beat me. Not this time. Now tell me where is Zandr."

"Oh, is little Thumbelina in love with the young fairy prince?"

"That is none of your business. Tell me where he is." She kept her gaze on the woman, but in the back of her mind she feared that the shape-shifter was stalling. For what? Violet wasn't sure if she wanted to know.

One thing was for certain. She had not seen a trace of either Zandr or Osric. That worried her. Where were they? The shape-shifter was doing a good job at irritating Violet by not giving a straight answer. She just hoped that Zandr was okay. *He can take care of himself. The most important thing is to stay focused on finding a way to break the curse before time runs out.*

With that thought in mind, Violet summoned a large gust of wind and pinned her opponent against the wall. No more games. She would make the shape-shifter talk one way or another. For the sake of everyone.

Chapter 66

"If you refuse to tell me about Zandr's whereabouts then perhaps you'd like to have a chat regarding the curse and how to break it." Violet narrowed her eyes at the woman who smirked back.

"It's too late for that. The curse is now permanent," the shape-shifter sneered.

"Liar."

"Do you believe that with all your heart? You wasted your time on me. The world is now doomed thanks to your own ignorance."

Violet studied the red head for a moment. There was something she was leaving out. The question was what? "Maybe I should tie you up and look for whatever it was you used to create the curse then smash it."

The shape-shifter laughed as everything around Violet faded into mist. Alone, and terrified, Violet walked through the void, with one single goal; to find the way out.

"Trickery isn't going to get you anywhere!" She winced as her voice carried on in an echo. Was this real or was she experiencing another illusion? Whatever was happening, she didn't like it.

"Now what am I going to do? I can't fail. Not like this." She turned around then frowned at finding herself back in the corridor of the Sky Fortress. "What?"

"Thumbelina? Are you all right?" Zandr glanced at her in concern.

She blinked up at him. "I- but… I wasn't here before…"

"What are you talking about? You've been standing there this entire time debating on which way to go. Are you feeling well? Perhaps the flight tired you out worse than you thought."

"No, I'm fine. I just…" She pivoted on her heels and froze. Somehow she was back in the room with the shape-shifter. "What is going on? What did you do to me?"

The woman laughed. "Me? I have done nothing to you. Have you ever considered that you are simply mad?"

Violet whirled around to confront her, but everything changed yet again. This time she was outside walking alongside Zandr.

"I miss the birds," he murmured.

"Birds… they're gone?"

He nodded. "Another part of the curse."

She bit her lip. "How long ago was that? How did they disappear?"

Zandr scowled at her questions. "I don't know. It has been awhile."

"Give me an exact date!"

"Are you all right? You're acting odd."

"Just tell me." Her heart hammered in her chest. This was wrong. It was all wrong. "It's all a lie. None of this is real."

"Thumbelina… have you lost your mind? Of course this is real!"

She drew back. "No. This is all in my mind. Everything is jumbled together. Or maybe it's not all in my mind after all and some of this has leaked into reality distorting it as well."

The fairy prince narrowed his gaze at her. "None of what you say makes sense…"

"Because you aren't real. It's all fake. Now I know what I have to do," with that she ran off leaving Zandr calling out after her.

Chapter 67

After what felt like several minutes of running, Violet came to a halt. She had no idea where to go or what she was looking for. All she knew was that she was somehow trapped in some sort of labyrinth of illusions. Her frustration levels boiled over when after taking several steps through the forest she was back underground clothed in the much loathed wedding gown. That was the last place she wanted to be.

Not caring what happened, she used a burst of wind to knock the door down. Once she stepped outside it, however, she was found herself perched precariously on the lily pad surrounded by toads. "No, this isn't right either! Think, Violet. There has to be a way out of here."

She hesitated a moment then stepped off the lily pad. Rather than feel the rush of the crisp river water, she instead landed in a flower garden.

Violet looked up and felt her eyes sting. Standing over her was a kind woman with soft blonde hair tied back in a ponytail.

"There is my little girl," she murmured, delight in her kind eyes at the sight of her tiny charge.

"Mama." Violet choked on the words then lowered her head. She knew she hadn't come into the world by normal means. She was a simple wish of a woman who couldn't bear children. Despite that the woman was still Mama. She smiled recalling the first time they had met. She was born from a magical flower. Her name was Thumbelina, but her nickname was Violet.

"The witch killed you. I'm sorry that I couldn't save you."

"Don't be silly, dear. I'm right here."

"No, you aren't. I'm sorry. We both lost so much on the day that I was stolen away. I shall always love you. Goodbye."

Before her mama could reply, Violet squeezed her eyes shut and turned hard on her toes. When she looked up, she found herself back on the roof of the Sky Fortress —the place where the maze had begun. "It's got to be in here somewhere. It's time to put an end to all of this insanity."

She wiped the tears from her eyes. She didn't bother changing back into her pink dress. Somehow the wedding gown seemed appropriate for the occasion. It would all end here.

She brushed past Zandr without a word and opened the door. Unlike the first time, when she came across the fork, she took the left one. She walked briskly, then came to a halt in horror as she found herself in what resembled a church. The large room was filled with pews. Light from the brilliant stain glass windows shown onto the aisles.

Violet struggled to breathe as music began to play. Her first instinct was to race out the door screaming. Instead she walked down the aisle. Brief glimpses of color from the windows stole her attention every once in a while as she moved.

Osric gave her a smug smile once she joined him at the altar. He said something that Violet didn't catch. Instead her attention continued to return to the windows. She frowned at the tinkling of glass. There was something odd about them.

Without a word she stepped away from him then turned to the windows. Her amber eyes widened at the sight of the birds, flowers, animals, and fairies that decorated them. Images of her life, she realized.

A slow smile crept across her lips. This had to be what she was looking for. It made sense. If she fulfilled the marriage in the heart of the illusion, it would seal it into reality. She would doom everyone, not just herself.

Violet closed her eyes forming her bow in her hands. She faced the largest window, staring into her own face depicted in glass. She drew back the string as an arrow appeared, then with a single wish to undo everything that the witch had done, released it.

Chapter 68

Glass exploded in front of Violet as shards of colors rained down on the floor. When nothing else happened, she frowned. Why didn't it work? She shouldn't still be in this room. She should be someplace else. It didn't make sense!

"Are you done with your little hissy fit?" The shape-shifter chastised.

Violet wasn't surprised to find that they were the only two in the room. "Break your spell now! I want no part in this."

"How naïve of you to believe that it would be that easy."

"I'm not letting you destroy this world. I will find a way to defeat you."

"My, big words from such a small girl. I could crush you like a bug if I were my normal size," the woman snorted.

Violet glared at her. "But you won't, because that's not as much fun as tormenting me. You need someone to play with to give your miserable existence any meaning."

"You horrible-"

"So I am right. That was just a guess, however, you just now confirmed it." She smiled, satisfied to have been able to best the witch at least a small amount. Violet glanced at the remaining windows then turned back to the pieces of the smashed one. "Is it that simple?"

Ignoring the witch's insults she walked to one of the remaining windows. If she included the large one at the very front, there were seven windows. Her brow narrowed as her mind went back to the Crystal Garden. Six pedestals. It might be just be some sort of strange coincidence…

"What are you doing?" the shape-shifter inquired as Violet walked to the center of the room.

"Breaking the curse." She released her bow into thin air then brought her hands together, drawing as much energy as she could handle. When she felt as though she could burst, she released it all around her. The remaining windows shattered upon impact. Rather than allow them to crash to the floor, she used her wind magic to gather every fragment with a gentle sweep.

"Stop! You must not do that!" The witch cried out, but her words were unheeded.

Violet used her full concentration to put together the shards like a jigsaw puzzle creating a new image. Once she fitted the last remaining piece, a brilliant light flooded the room. The woman screamed as she shattered like fine crystal. Violet stared up at the new window —her own eyes stared back at her.

She gave it a sad smile as she used her last bit of magic to summon her bow and an arrow. No matter what happened, this was the right thing to do. With that thought in mind, she fired the arrow. The world around her burst then disappeared.

Chapter 69

Violet clasped her hands to her chest as she closed her eyes. The Sky Fortress had faded like a dream when she had shattered the curse. That also resulted in the enchanted cloud to lose the ability to support the weight of even a sewing needle, sending the weak girl plummeting to the ground below.

She could feel herself falling, but was unable to do anything to stop herself. She had used up too much energy in breaking the curse to be able to summon her wings let alone a pillow of air. Was death going to swoop in and claim her? Was this her end? At least the curse was broken at last. She wouldn't die in vain. She would miss Zandr and the other fairies, but Zandr most of all. If only she could use a bit of her air magic to slow her descent, but that alone might kill her. At least she didn't fail. That was something to be happy about, right? If only she could see Zandr once last time.

"I will see you soon, Mama."

Her breath caught as something snatched her out of the heavens. Amber eyes flew open as she stared in wonder at a pair of silver ones. "Zandr."

"Did you really think I would allow you to fall to your death?" His lips quirked into a small smile. "Hang on tight. I'll have to move fast since I'm not used to flying in human form. Thank you, by the way. You did it."

That's right, she was human sized once again. She smiled back, hugging him tight. "I almost killed myself in the process, but you're welcome. Thank you for coming to my rescue."

"We're just getting to know one another. I couldn't let you die yet."

Violet wasn't sure how to respond to that. "Well, thank you."

"You're too important to me."

Her heart skipped a beat from his words as they landed. To her surprise he refused to put her down. "I didn't break anything if that is what you are wondering."

"Right, but you are still weak otherwise you would have flown back to the earth on your own. You never struck me as the type to engage in death-defying stunts."

"I guess you know me better than you thought." She rested her head on his shoulder, content to remain in his arms, at least for now then lost consciousness.

Chapter 70

Amber eyes fluttered open then blinked. Violet was amazed to find herself in the most enchanted looking room she had ever seen. Crystal ornaments were dangling from sconces throughout the room. Beautiful handmade tapestries decorated the walls. She was delighted to see that many of them depicted flowers.

How did she get there? She couldn't recall, but had a feeling that she was in the fairy castle. She looked out the window and smiled at the sight of the glorious waterfall.

"You're awake."

Her face brightened as Zandr stepped into the room. She pushed herself to a sitting position then smiled at seeing she was no longer wearing the horrid wedding gown but had somehow switched back to her pink one. "And alive thanks to you."

"How do you feel?"

"A bit achy, but nothing too bad. I guess you brought me here?"

He shrugged. "My parents insisted. Plus, it was the closest place."

I see." Violet chewed her lip, feeling rather awkward. She was just a regular girl—Normal sized for a change she realized, but ordinary. "I guess I should be off then."

"Why? You saved all of us." Zandr reached over and lifted one of her strawberry blonde curls from her face. He twisted it in his fingers as an almost after-thought. "They are proud of you. All of us are. We are still alive because of you, not to mention have re-gained our ability to make ourselves human-sized again."

"That's good I guess."

He chuckled. "Yes, my sister is now dancing around because she can fit into all her gowns again."

"I bet that is quite a sight."

"It is indeed. She would like to meet you as does the rest of my family."

Family. That word brought to mind a certain arro-gant fairy prince. "What became of Osric?"

Zandr sobered at the mentioning of his power-hungry brother. "He's been imprisoned for committing treason. Everyone is very distraught over his plans to overthrow the kingdom. He's been plotting it for months. We have discovered that he planned to either kill or enslave us all."

"I'm sorry that he was so deceitful," Violet mur-mured. Even though she had no siblings, she imagined that to have a family member turn on everyone was quite painful.

The fairy prince grabbed her hand. "Let's put that horrendous experience behind us. I have something I wish to show you first."

"Okay." With her simple word of acceptance, Vio-let found herself whisked out of the beautiful room, down the hall, and out the door. What she saw next seemed to light up her eyes like the sun.

Chapter 71

Violet squealed in delight at the sight of flowers in every color imaginable growing throughout the lush garden. A dreamy fragrance wafted through the air making her sigh in happiness. She didn't think she had ever seen so many flowers before in her entire life! "This is incredible! I feel like I've died and gone to heaven."

"I'm glad you are still among the living," Zandr chuckled at her enthusiasm. "I thought you would enjoy visiting here first."

"You guessed correct."

Violet knew she shouldn't. He was a fairy prince and she was human girl. But there he was. Dark tousled hair. Unreal polished silver eyes. He never once tried to control her unlike many she had come across. However, they were of two separate worlds. It didn't makes sense. It couldn't work. But there she was. And there he was. It was the perfect situation yet, just the thought of it made her feel guilty. There was no way it would work out. He might already be engaged. She was a peasant. Even if he felt the same way his parents probably wouldn't approve. Plus, why was she even thinking about romance? Whenever that subject was breeched she always ran. Too many times she had a matchmaker who believed that they knew what was best for her. Because of that, Violet always refused any mentioning of the word love.

But now… Things seemed different. What was her heart trying to tell her? Was it her imagination or did he seem to share the same feelings? It was so confusing. She was being silly. It was all wishful thinking. Nothing more. Yet when he looked at her, she could feel her heart leap with excitement. It was too hard to ignore, this rush of feelings.

"Thumbelina?"

Then again, he couldn't seem to call her by anything more than that name.

"It's Violet." She made a face as the memory of the two names surfaced. "Actually it's both, but I prefer Violet."

"Then I shall try to remember to call you by that name."

She nodded, satisfied. "What is it you wanted to say?"

"You…" He faltered. "Nothing."

"Okay."

Was he nervous? It seemed unlikely since he always carried off a cool and collected demeanor. Violet tried to shrug it off. He grabbed her arm.

She turned to look at him when he captured her mouth with his in a kiss. She froze, unable to believe what was happening. Was Zandr, the fairy prince, really kissing her? Why? He didn't seem the type to fall head over heels for a girl like her. It was just ludicrous! She imaged that it would start snowing cake any minute now…

But it didn't. His lips were still against hers, warm and caressing. One of his hands was pressed to her back. Then the next second he drew away.

"I apologize. I do not know what came over me…"

"It's okay," she managed to squeak out. "I… kind of liked it."

Violet kicked herself for such a lame response.

He spun around to look at her. His face was awash with shock. "You did? You mean you…"

"Yes? I mean, if you meant, do I feel the same way… I do." To prove it, Violet was shocked to find herself tugging the bewildered prince to her and pressing her lips against his. He returned the kiss with a bit more force before they broke it off.

Violet covered her face with her hands. "I can't believe I just did that! You're a prince for crying out loud! I'm nobody."

"No, you aren't. You're special."

"If you mean in that definition that means dumb then, yeah I'll agree with you there."

"No." He took her hands in his. "My being a prince is meaningless. I will never be king therefore it doesn't matter who I choose."

Violet's stomach turned as a queasy sensation filled her. "About that… I can't. I can't marry you!"

Before he could react she broke free of his grip and ran as terror gained control of her emotions. She was tired of marriage proposals. Frog, mole, human, fairy… she didn't care. She refused to marry anyone! It just wasn't going to happen. Not to her. She didn't want to get married. Not now. Maybe not ever.

"Wait!"

She could hear Zandr's heavy footsteps behind her. She squeezed her eyes shut, willing her wings to appear, but he had grabbed her from behind before she could take off to the sky.

"Let go of me!" She wiggled in his grasp, but he kept his hold secure.

"No, you need to listen to me."

"I'm not going to marry you!"

"That's not what I was going to ask you."

She stilled. "But it sounded like…"

Zandr shook his head. "What I was trying to say is that I have the right to choose whoever I want when the time comes. I don't mean today or tomorrow. Someday. However no one can say otherwise that I have to marry another royal. It's my choice alone."

Violet stared in bewilderment at Zandr. Did he really say what she thought he did? "But I said…"

He took her hands before she could run. "I don't mean marriage. That is too much for my taste, at least at this stage. We just met after all. However, I would like to get to know you more."

Violet chewed on her lip. "I… wow. I did not expect this. I mean you never seemed to show any interest in me before… This is quite sudden."

"I promise not to push you into anything you don't want, including marriage."

She smiled at his sincere words. "If you mean that then okay. We'll give being in a relationship a shot. Who knows? It might be good for both of us."

"Really?"

She could feel a blush warm her cheeks. "I have gotten a bit attached to you. After all, unlike anyone else that was in my life, you never tried to make me do something that I didn't want to."

He lifted her chin up with one hand and pressed his lips to hers in a gentle kiss.

Violet jolted out of surprise then warmed into it. Perhaps dating him wouldn't be so bad after all despite the fact that he was a bit tricky to read. "Slow?"

"I don't think I could handle fast if I wanted to."

She laughed at his words. "That makes me very happy to hear."

He picked her up and spun her around in the air.

"You are just full of surprises!"

"Glad you approve."

Chapter 72

"Relax, they're not going to hate you. You have already met my parents after all," Zandr whispered in Violet's ear as they approached the throne room.

The strawberry blonde girl bobbed her head, too afraid that her voice might come out in a squeak. She struggled to keep herself from fidgeting. An hour ago she would have been fine, but after kissing Zandr… everything seemed to change. Now she was anticipating disapproval more than ever. She was an orphan so it wasn't like she had anything that a king or queen would deem worthy of dating their son.

Why did she have to kiss him back? Things were so much simpler when they were in a platonic relationship, not… whatever they were now.

What was she going to say? What were they going to say? Butterflies swarmed her stomach as a multitude of possible outcomes flooded her mind. She hoped she wasn't going to get sick.

Breathe, Violet urged herself as they crossed the threshold into the throne room. There was no turning back now.

What she didn't anticipate was a young woman with hair the same shade as Zandr's, to run towards her, then envelope her in a bone crushing hug. "Thank you so very much! You are my hero!"

"You're welcome," Violet replied, feeling quite awkward at the unexpected embrace.

"Keeva, let the girl breath, please," her mother scolded from her place on the throne.

The princess flushed, but released the petite strawberry blonde. "My apologies. You just don't understand how miserable it has been being stuck at fairy size when most of my things are human-sized."

"It's okay and it's nice to meet you."

Zandr took Violet's arm then ushered her towards his parents.

The Fairy King and Queen both bowed their heads in respect. The king was the first to speak. "We thank you for all that you have done for us in breaking the horrible curse. We are in your debt."

Violet clasped her hands together. "It is not a problem. It was my destiny I guess you could say."

"We also know that you have been orphaned due to that shape-shifter. To show our gratitude, we would be honored for you to call this your home."

"What? I can't I-"

"We have more than enough room. In fact the room you had awoken in is now yours," the queen explained. "Although we cannot bring your mother back, we can provide you with the comforts of home. You can think of us as a second family."

Violet bit her lip. She didn't know what to say or if she should accept. Everything was happening so fast that she felt like she'd wind up with whiplash trying to keep up. "I don't know. I mean I still have a quest to complete and will have to leave tomorrow."

"Then think about it, please. Just know that there is a place where you belong."

"All right. I will."

The king cleared his throat. "We shall provide you with supplies for your journey as well. I trust that Zandr will be accompanying you?"

"Yes," the prince replied before Violet could say a word.

"Very good. We will pray for a safe journey and pray for your return in the morning. For now, we shall have a great feast and celebrate the end of the nightmare!"

Violet found herself smiling. The choice was hers on what she wished to do when she returned, but still, she had a place to return to. That made her feel happy.

"There is no pressure," Zandr whispered in her ear.

"I know. And I think that's why I might say yes... after we return of course."

He slid his hand into hers and squeezed it. "It sounds like a good plan."

Chapter 73

*V*iolet gazed up at the sky. She sensed Zandr move to her side. She closed her eyes as the wind tousled her hair. "Have you ever wondered what would have happened if the curse had never been cast?"

"Not really."

"Do you think we'd be standing here at the moment if it hadn't happened?"

"Maybe. Maybe not. We probably will never know."

Perhaps it's better that way." Her mind drifted to the shape-shifter. Ever since Violet had broken the spell, the woman who had kidnapped her hadn't been seen from since. There was a possibility that the spell had been woven with the witch's soul and that once it broke, she too met her demise. Either way, Violet hoped to never have to hear from her ever again.

Pushing those thoughts away, she turned to Zandr with a grin. "When we return I want to make the most beautiful flower garden ever!"

Zandr frowned, "Is there something wrong with the one I showed you?"

"No, I love it. I just always wanted to make my own. Plus, you can never have too many flowers."

"If that is what will make you happy, I will help."

She felt wonderful. Zandr's family accepted her as one of their own despite the fact that marriage was a long ways away if it was ever to occur. To her joy, the king and queen were fine with that idea. They also provided the supplies needed for the long journey. Zandr insisted on accompanying her, which she couldn't argue against. She preferred not having to travel alone.

Violet gave his hand a squeeze, glad to have him by her side. "Then we should head off now. I don't know how long it will take us to find Lunette or the others."

"Might be easier to go by hawk."

Her eyes widened. "We can do that?"

"You are a fairy after all."

"No, I'm not, I'm just a-"

"You have wings the same as me. You're just a little more unique which makes you a lot more interesting. Don't make me argue with you on this."

Violet bit her lip then nodded. "All right. Hawk it is!"

Zandr gave a whistle as a beautiful silver colored bird flew towards them. The hawk circled once then landed on the fairy prince's outstretched arm. "He's safe. You can pet him if you'd like."

"Okay," she lifted a hesitant hand to the bird and stroked the silky feathers. "Will you be able to direct him to where we need to go?"

"Yes, and when Sterling tires, he can perch on my shoulder as we walk. We have a bond."

"I see. Then I guess the sooner we head out, the better. After all, there is no telling how long this journey might take."

Zandr nodded as he set the bird down on the ground. He looked at Violet and smiled. "Ready when you are."

She squeezed her eyes shut, willing herself to shrink. When she opened them, she laughed at the sight of Sterling towering over her. "It worked!"

"Congratulations," the fairy prince laughed as he lifted her up. The bird bowed, allowing the two fairies to climb onto his back. "Hold on tight. Taking off can be a little shaky at times."

"Okay," Violet gripped the bird's feathers as Zandr held her close.

"Don't worry, I won't let you fall."

She gasped as Sterling flapped his wings in preparation to take to the air before finally doing so. She giggled in merriment at the rush of flying on a bird's back. She didn't think she had ever felt so happy before in her life. Her thoughts drifted towards the other chosen of the Crystal Garden as well as Grace. She hoped to be able to help grant them the same joy she felt at that moment someday. That was a promise she longed to keep.

About the Author

LJ Gastineau lives in Saint Augustine, Florida, and is a graduate of the University of Central Florida. She is one of three authors for the website, TrinityGateways.net, and is a co-founder for Trinity Gateways LLC. *Frozen Reflection* and *Quaking Tower* are her first two published Young Adult novels. LJ also has a short horror story entitled *Doll's House* that was published in two adult anthologies: *Dark Things II* from Pill Hill Press and *Shadows of the Mind* from Trinity Gateways LLC.

She is currently working on the fourth book of her *Crystal Garden Saga* series, *Drowned Voice,* as well as her cross-genre serial entitled *Hidden Mystique,* which is available exclusively on the website, JukePop Serials.

More from

The

Crystal Garden

Saga

The saga begins with

Frozen Reflection
Book 1 of the Crystal Garden Saga

By LJ Gastineau

This would be a birthday she would never forget.

Most girls look forward to their sweet sixteenth birthday. For Bianca Flynn, she believed hers would be an average celebration, one where she would be stuck at home with the stepmother she dislikes. Then things start happening. A strange reaction to apples and an odd phobia of mirrors quickly spirals out of control, throwing her into a world that she thought only existed in stories. So what if she resembles a certain dark haired, pale skinned princess? Fairy tales weren't real. Right?

A mystical quest was not the gift she expected.

After all it isn't everyday that you are swept into a land cursed by a spell that can only be broken with the power of a crystal rose. And there is only one who can fulfill that task, the Princess Snow White.

Turning sixteen has never been more adventurous.

Quaking Tower

Book 2 of the Crystal Garden Saga

By LJ Gastineau

You don't have to dwell in a tower to be isolated.

Cybele Lockley should know. To say that she lived a sheltered life would be an understatement. For as long as she could remember, she had been stuck in a rural house in the middle of nowhere, separated from the world due to a medical condition. Her only company was her grandmother, and just in the morning and the evenings. During the day, she was forbidden to leave the house or even look out the tiny windows. Longing to be free of the isolation, Cybele created a make-believe world in an old notebook, filled with the romance and adventure of a character based on the fairy tale of Rapunzel.

She thought it was just a story…

Everything changes when she attempts to cut her hair for the first time. The room spins, her tawny colored locks grew to nearly three times their original length, the house is transformed into a woodland cottage, and the landscape morphs to resemble an imaginary setting from her notebook. Now she must work to find her true reality – and in doing so must assume the role of her make-believe heroine and complete a quest to find a crystal rose.

This Rapunzel isn't just letting down her hair.

Drowned Voice

Book 4 of the Crystal Garden Saga

By LJ Gastineau

What she loves most combines into one

stunning talent…

Mirielle Riva grew up in the foster care system, migrating from one home to another with no family to call her own. She fought the loneliness by indulging in her favorite things whenever, however, she could: dancing and the water. Now a teenager in high school, she finds a ray of happiness when she lands a place on the school's varsity swim team.

…with unusual consequences…

Her sixteenth birthday arrives with little fanfare. For Mirielle, it's just another day of swim team practice at the school's summer camp. The only notable blight is she's lost her voice. Though unable to speak, she attends practice anyway. All goes well until when she surfaces she discovers she is no longer in the world she'd woken in that morning.

…and a price that she never anticipated having to pay.

Still without a voice, she finds herself in a cursed kingdom being ravaged by the sea. With the waters rising, she must seek out answers if she has any hope of returning to the world she'd left behind. Doing so will pit her against pirates, sea creatures, and royalty with no way to know who is friend or foe – and she soon discovers that what she knew of the mermaid's tale will be of little help to her here. There wasn't anything about a crystal rose in the original story, after all…

Mirielle will soon learn that some legends are far more real than she'd believed – and some happy endings aren't written, but are forged in adversity.

This little mermaid fights back.

Coming Soon

in the

Summer of 2014